# A CITY OF LIES

---

## A SHADE OF VAMPIRE 55

### BELLA FORREST

The Gender End (Book 7)

A SHADE OF VAMPIRE SERIES

**Series 1: Derek & Sofia's story**

A Shade of Vampire (Book 1)

A Shade of Blood (Book 2)

A Castle of Sand (Book 3)

A Shadow of Light (Book 4)

A Blaze of Sun (Book 5)

A Gate of Night (Book 6)

A Break of Day (Book 7)

**Series 2: Rose & Caleb's story**

A Shade of Novak (Book 8)

A Bond of Blood (Book 9)

A Spell of Time (Book 10)

A Chase of Prey (Book 11)

A Shade of Doubt (Book 12)

A Turn of Tides (Book 13)

A Dawn of Strength (Book 14)

A Fall of Secrets (Book 15)

An End of Night (Book 16)

**Series 3: The Shade continues with a new hero...**

A Wind of Change (Book 17)

A Trail of Echoes (Book 18)

A Throne of Fire (Book 40)

A Tide of War (Book 41)

**Series 6: A Gift of Three**

A Gift of Three (Book 42)

A House of Mysteries (Book 43)

A Tangle of Hearts (Book 44)

A Meet of Tribes (Book 45)

A Ride of Peril (Book 46)

A Passage of Threats (Book 47)

A Tip of Balance (Book 48)

A Shield of Glass (Book 49)

A Clash of Storms (Book 50)

**Series 7: A Call of Vampires**

A Call of Vampires (Book 51)

A Valley of Darkness (Book 52)

A Hunt of Fiends (Book 53)

A Den of Tricks (Book 54)

A City of Lies (Book 55)

A SHADE OF DRAGON TRILOGY

A Shade of Dragon 1

A Shade of Dragon 2

A Shade of Dragon 3

A SHADE OF KIEV TRILOGY

A Shade of Kiev 1

A Shade of Kiev 2

A Shade of Kiev 3

THE SECRET OF SPELLSHADOW MANOR

(Completed series)

The Secret of Spellshadow Manor (Book 1)

The Breaker (Book 2)

The Chain (Book 3)

The Keep (Book 4)

The Test (Book 5)

The Spell (Book 6)

BEAUTIFUL MONSTER DUOLOGY

Beautiful Monster 1

Beautiful Monster 2

DETECTIVE ERIN BOND (Adult thriller/mystery)

Lights, Camera, GONE

Write, Edit, KILL

For an updated list of Bella's books, please visit her website: www.bellaforrest.net

Join Bella's VIP email list and she'll send you an email reminder as soon as her next book is out: www.forrestbooks.com

# NEW GENERATION LIST

- **Avril (vampire):** adopted daughter of Lucas and biological daughter of Marion.
- **Blaze (fire dragon):** son of fire dragons Heath and Athena.
- **Caia (part fae/human):** daughter of Grace and Lawrence.
- **Fiona (vampire):** daughter of Benedict (son of Rose and Caleb) and Yelena.
- **Harper (sentry/vampire):** daughter of Hazel and Tejus.
- **Scarlett (vampire):** daughter of Jeramiah (son of Lucas Novak) and Pippa (daughter of Cameron Hendry).

# FAMILY TREE

If you'd like to check out the Novaks' family tree, visit: www.forrestbooks.com/tree

# 1

## BLAZE

King Shaytan left us in the meranium box with a small barrel of water and the promise that we would be looked after. As if that made any difference.

Caia and I were prisoners, trapped, at the mercy of the king of daemons. My blood boiled as I paced the small box, while Caia leaned her back against one of the walls. Our reflections were blurry on the shiny metal surface, and my steps echoed in the small tunnel through which Shaytan had pushed our water. The box was approximately three by three meters, its walls at least ten meters thick, completely sealed and with nothing but that little tunnel connecting us to the outside world—even Caia couldn't fit through it.

We didn't even know if Harper, Caspian, Hansa, and Jax had made it out alive.

"What do we do?" Caia murmured, her gaze fixed on the floor.

It wasn't the first time she had asked that question. She seemed lost, and it tore me apart on the inside to see her so distraught and vulnerable.

"For now, all we can do is get a little bit of rest," I replied. "Just to clear our heads and get ready for what comes next."

"What exactly is coming next?" Caia asked. "I mean, we are stuck here. We cannot use our fire to get out. Whatever this meranium metal does, it includes stifling our only weapon against these daemons. On top of that, we have no idea where the others are, if they even made it out, if they're okay... and let's not forget that if you try to go full dragon, I'm going to get crushed in the process. So what comes next?"

She was frustrated, and I couldn't exactly blame her—I felt the same. But I wasn't going to let her fall prey to whatever the daemons had in store for us, and I certainly wasn't going to let her succumb to any kind of panic or, worse, hopelessness.

I stopped, then turned to face her, and I felt my heart swell painfully with the need to hold her. She looked up at me, her teal eyes wide and glazed with tears.

"Let's take it one step at a time, Caia," I said. "We won't be in here forever. If the others are out there, they will come for us."

"But do they know where we are?"

"I'm sure they will find out, one way or another," I replied, feeling the confidence return to my voice. "Besides, we are most likely inside the palace. They will figure it out. Harper's relentless, you know that. She will stop at nothing to get you back."

"To get *us* back." She gave me a weak smile.

"Sure." I shrugged, feigning disinterest. "To get *us* back. But we both know I'm not the one she's besties with."

At least she still had the strength to smile, and even chuckle. It meant that there was still hope, not just for her, but for the both of us, because she was my anchor and I was hers.

"And what if..." Her expression changed from a mild half-smile to a deep, shadowy frown as she choked up. "What if they didn't make it? What if... What if we are stuck here? At Shaytan's mercy... What are we going to do then?"

I let a long and heavy sigh roll out of my chest, my shoulders dropping. I struggled to find a positive outcome in all of this. There was no way I was going to rot in here, and there certainly wasn't any way that I would let Caia spend the rest of her life in a meranium box.

"Still, they won't keep us in here forever," I replied. "They will have to let us out at some point, whether it'll be to put me in chains, or to transfer us to some other larger, equally charmed box. We both know by now that they probably possess enough swamp witch magic to restrain my dragon abilities in the long term. I can't be sure, at this point, but given what we've seen so far, I can speculate."

"So, what? We just wait for a good opening?" she asked, and I didn't miss that tinge of sarcasm in her tone.

However, we were suddenly interrupted. The latch at the end of the small tunnel opened with a loud clang. Both Caia and I immediately moved to the opening to see who was out there.

"Oh, hello, pets." The daemon sneered, narrowing his red eyes at us. He wasn't a regular grunt, judging by his heavy leather tunic and the gold thread woven around his horns, which stretched down and backward. His long black hair was smooth and tightly braided on the sides, each lock ending in a cluster of beads. He was royalty, and he looked familiar.

"Who are you?" I asked, my tone rough, my anger audible.

He chuckled, carefully analyzing Caia and me, as if we were zoo exhibits.

"I suppose it's only fair that you know the name of your... caretaker," the daemon replied. "I am Mammon, son of Shaytan."

"Our caretaker?" Caia shot back, raising an eyebrow, unable to hide her contempt.

"Well, yes," Mammon replied, then pushed a small wooden tray through the tunnel. It didn't go all the way to the end, where we stood, so I had to reach out and pull it toward us. It held two warm steel dishes. They had actually made an effort to provide us with food. "As you can see, I am taking care of you. Therefore, I am your caretaker. Although, to be fair, I would much rather eat your souls than feed you, but Father says you are not to be touched yet."

He didn't seem happy with that decision, but I couldn't say

I was bothered. On the contrary, it meant that Shaytan needed us alive and in one piece, for whatever reason.

"So what are we doing here?" I asked.

Mammon rolled his eyes, as if he couldn't be bothered to answer such basic questions.

"You two have no idea what you've gotten yourselves into," he scoffed. "You don't even know half of what is really going on, but you sure are keen to ask the most unnecessary questions. Do you really think it matters why *you* are here? Because, frankly, you should both know that this is where you end. So is it even worth it to ask why?"

"Okay, smartass," Caia retorted, "how about we try another question? Such as, what *is* really going on here?"

Mammon chuckled, slowly shaking his head. My only wish was that my arms were long enough for me to reach out and snap his neck like a chicken's. Fire raged through me, fueled by my inability to get myself and Caia out of this mess.

"Now that is a question that I would love to answer, but I can't," he said.

"Then why did you mention it?" She scowled at him.

"Purely for the joy of messing with you, of course."

I snapped. My throat burned, and I released a thick river of fire through the tunnel. I still had my blazing breath, though it had no physical impact on the meranium box itself. Mammon went pale for a split second, then swiftly shut the latch tight before my flames could reach him.

A couple of seconds went by. Both Caia and I stared at the darkness of the sealed tunnel.

"Okay, so, maybe if you try that again, but faster, so they don't expect it, we might have a shot?" Caia looked at me, raising her eyebrows and pursing her lips.

"I'm not sure that will work again." I frowned. "Mammon will probably be more careful the next time he pops by."

A few minutes passed, and the latch opened again. We stilled. It wasn't Mammon this time. Based on the gold thread woven around his horns, this was another prince, but none of the ones I'd seen at the earlier gathering. I couldn't help but wonder if I could try that fire breath trick again. Perhaps I could wait another minute, and just gauge his reflexes. I couldn't risk exhibiting a habit for which they could be prepared, going forward.

"And who are *you*?" I said.

"I was wondering who my brother was talking to earlier. It looked kind of weird from the outside," the daemon prince replied. "As if he were talking to a hole in a wall. For a second, I thought he'd lost his mind."

"Who the hell are you? What do you want?" Caia had run out of patience.

"Ah, you're that fire fae," the daemon shot back. "You can definitely hold your own in a fight. I watched you the day before, when you were looking for your friend in the gorges. It's a shame you ended up in here."

"You were in the gorge yesterday?" She frowned. "You still haven't answered my question. *Who are you?*"

"I'm the one who gave your friend back to you," he replied.

It dawned on me then who we were talking to. This was the daemon that had abducted Fiona.

"You're Zane," I breathed. That was even more confusing, looking back. What was a prince doing around Azure Heights? Most importantly, what was he doing kidnapping our friend? "You're a prince."

"That, unfortunately, I am. And you're a dragon, stuck in a box." He snorted.

"Yeah, the irony does not escape me either," I muttered.

"Hold on," Caia replied, "so, if you're a prince, why did you release Fiona? And why don't you release us, while you're here?"

"Whoa, whoa, whoa." Zane lifted his hands in a dismissive gesture. "First of all, whatever I do with Fiona is my business, and mine alone. Second, I am not getting involved in whatever... this is. I do my best to stay out of the king's business."

"But you're a prince. You sit on the Council. You *are* part of the king's business," Caia said.

"Well, aren't you perceptive," Zane scoffed. "It's true, I do sit on the Council, and I'm impressed that you know that, but I do not try to interfere much. I just cast my vote whenever my brothers push for some new law. So, yes, technically speaking, I am part of the king's business, as you so bluntly put it, but not as much as you might think."

"But you chose to release Fiona." Caia didn't give up. "That makes me think that you're not half as bad as the rest of your... family. Help us get out of here. Otherwise, Fiona will come looking for us, along with the others."

"Listen, if I were you, I would be more worried about your situation." Zane adopted a nonchalant demeanor. "I'm not getting involved. I'll think about it, at best."

He then closed the latch, depriving us of the opportunity to further try to convince him to help us. Caia then looked at me, concern drawing shadows between her eyebrows. As dire as our situation was at this point, I still couldn't ignore the magnetism charging the air around us.

"Clearly," I said, trying to focus on what had just happened, "Zane is pretty much entitled to watch out for himself before anyone else. It is difficult for me to see him just dropping everything to help us. I'm guessing the wrath of Shaytan could be as deadly to him as to anyone else."

"Fair point." Caia sighed. "But still, it's worth a shot. He did say he'd think about it. Let's see if he does."

We didn't have any other option. We were stuck here, with just a few feet of space to move through. I placed my hands on her shoulders, squeezing gently as a reassuring gesture. My intention was to keep her calm, but all I managed to do was rile myself up. Our eyes met, and I realized exactly how small this meranium box was.

We had plenty of time to kill before we would see Zane again, I figured, and that made me nervous, mainly because I was so close to her and I couldn't get away. To be honest, I didn't *want* to get away, but I feared that, sooner or later, I would find it harder and harder to hold onto my celibacy vow.

Even in this box, even in the middle of hell itself, Caia was the bright, shining star around whom I orbited, the one I needed to hold tight. Even now, I wondered what her lips would taste like.

*Yeah, I'm in for a rough ride...*

## 2

### HARPER

(DAUGHTER OF HAZEL & TEJUS)

Caspian and I made our way through the city. We moved as fast as we could, sneaking through the dark and narrow alleys, avoiding the groups of daemons out looking for us. My stomach churned, and my feet felt heavy, but we had to get into Mose's hut before our invisibility spell wore off. It was bad enough that some of the daemons had red garnet lenses through which they could see us. We couldn't risk *all* of them seeing us.

I held Caspian's hand, as we kept turning left and right. He guided me through the slums until we made it to Mose's. He pulled the drapes over the entrance, and we both stood quietly for a while, until we became visible again.

My mind had gone into overdrive, trying to keep up with my body, as I adjusted to our new circumstances. Shaytan had seen us. None of us could have known that they could use red garnet to see those using the invisibility spell. In hindsight, though, it kind of made sense. I had a hard time imagining a throng of hunter daemons holding hands while they converged on their prey—we held hands in invisible form in order not to lose each other, or used vocal signals; the daemons would've had to do the same without those red lenses. At least we'd learned something new.

Caia and Blaze had been taken hostage by Shaytan and his hordes. Caspian had a point, though, that Shaytan was interested in keeping them alive. Therefore, we had *that* sort of working for us.

"There are so many things going through my head right now." I dropped to my knees, my limbs weak and tired. I could feel another wave of tears coming up, but I did my best to keep it down, broiling in the pit of my stomach. "We don't even know where Jax and Hansa are..."

Caspian moved across the room, then lowered himself in front of me, so we could be on the same level. He gripped my chin between his thumb and index finger, lifting my head slowly so he could look me in the eyes.

"They are both smart, cunning, and fast enough to outrun any of those beasts outside," he said, his voice low but somewhat reassuring. I swallowed hard, and gave him a soft nod in response.

"I wonder where they are."

To my surprise, I quickly got the answer to my question, as

the main entrance drapes moved. My hands reached for my swords, as two possibilities shot through my mind – daemons, or Jax and Hansa. Fortunately, the latter became visible as their invisibility spell wore off. I sprang to my feet and immediately pulled them into my arms, holding them both as close as I could. It felt as though I could breathe again.

"You have no idea how good it is to see you," I breathed. Jax and Hansa both responded to my hug, and tightened their arms around me. Hansa even dropped a kiss on the top of my head, before gently pushing me away so she could measure me from head to toe.

"Likewise, little vampire." She smiled softly. "I'm glad to see that you're in one piece. That you're *both* in one piece."

Caspian gave them a friendly nod, then sat by the now-dying fire we had left behind earlier. We joined him, welcoming the temporary comfort and quiet offered by Mose's hut.

"Where are Blaze and Caia? Have you seen them?" Jax asked.

Grief constricted my throat, and I choked up while trying to speak. Caspian put one hand on my knee, then filled them in for me.

"The daemons got them," he said. "They knocked them out, and they carried them inside the palace. My guess is that Shaytan wants them alive. Chances are he could use them as bait, to get us out of hiding."

It took Jax and Hansa some time to process the news. They

were both floored, but gradually snapped back to a more composed state. Watching them was enough to help me get back into the right mindset. We had a lot to do, and I needed a clear head.

"We're going to get them back," Hansa muttered, staring at the ashes in the fire pit.

Jax put his arm around her shoulders and pulled her to him, pressing his lips against her temple. It surprised me to see them so close. This was the ultimate shift in their dynamic: they were now closer than ever before. Weirdly, it had taken thousands of daemons chasing after us for them to get over whatever had stood between them in the first place.

"Rest assured, we're not leaving here without them," Jax replied softly.

I could feel my right eyebrow rising slowly as I stared at them. *Took you long enough...*

My only hope was that we would all make it out of the daemon city alive, so that Jax and Hansa could really take their relationship to the next level. I held hope that the universe wasn't cruel enough to end their story here, in the bowels of Neraka.

"What happened back there?" Hansa asked, looking at me. "What were those lenses?"

"It's red garnet," Caspian replied.

"They could see us through them," I added. "That was entirely unexpected. It was as if Shaytan knew we would be there, somehow. I saw him looking around, then straight at us, but I didn't think anything of it, since we were invisible. But then he started grinning... and I realized that he could see us. I swear, this is making less sense than before. The more we uncover, the less we know."

"We have to find a way to get Caia and Blaze out of there," Jax said. Hansa leaned into him. "We will have to find a way to infiltrate that palace."

"The parameters of our mission have changed," I replied. "We have daemons, some of them with red lenses through which they can see us. We have giant soldiers, or generals, or whatever they're called. We have pit wolves and death claws, along with everyone else who basically wants a piece of us. Yeah, count me in."

"Knowing you, Harper," Hansa smirked, "and how much you love a good challenge, I'm glad to see you so energized and eager to kick so many asses."

I felt the corner of my mouth twitch, mainly because she was right. I definitely looked forward to killing as many of those horned bastards as I could.

"At least we have morale going for us," Caspian said. "I'm sure that Miss Hellswan will get plenty of opportunities to burn all that energy."

His aura had a sheen of gold to it as he gave me a brief smile, his jade eyes fixed on mine. My cheeks burned, and my heart skipped a beat. He was right. I was going to get plenty of action in that palace, and many heads would fall in the process.

*You don't imprison my friends and expect to get away with it.*

Maybe most people who looked at Shaytan saw a giant, fearsome king. All I saw was my main enemy—and there was only one thing I did with my enemies. I crushed them. No matter how big.

# 3

## AVRIL

### (DAUGHTER OF LUCAS & MARION)

The world around me was kind and warm. Or, at least, that's what my dream felt like. My heart sang, as I gradually opened my eyes and realized that the warmth was not going away. I wasn't dreaming it. I could feel it.

A couple of seconds passed. I slowly adjusted my eyes to the semi-darkness of my room at the Broken Bow Inn. The shutters kept the sunlight out, but minuscule little rays still managed to sneak in, marking a handful of bright little dots on the wooden floor.

I was wrapped in a pair of strong arms, beneath the bedcover. My breath hitched as I remembered the night before —Heron coming to my room, awkwardly hanging around, falling asleep on the divan... I'd tried to tell him how I felt. But he was already sleeping deeply and didn't hear it. Instead, he got into bed with me later, and I slipped into dreamland in his embrace.

He stirred, and I felt his firm body against mine, every muscle and every sharp line perfectly molded to my curves. My temperature started to rise, as if the sun itself were hugging me. I feared I would burn, but at the same time, I couldn't let go. It felt too good to be true.

I could go over and over all the steps that had brought us to this point, but I wasn't able to identify the exact moment in which I had fallen so hard for Heron. The only certainty was that I had fallen for him, and had no idea how to deal with it... or get out of it. *This is such a sweet mess...*

Reality started to kick in, ever so slowly. As much as I wanted to, I couldn't stay like this forever. I needed to put some distance between us so that I could find the courage to tell Heron everything I had told him the night before... again. After a couple of deep breaths, I moved to get out of bed.

But Heron wasn't ready to let me go yet. He groaned and tightened his hold on me, his arms around my ribcage and his hands resting on my hips, as if I were a stuffed toy. Nevertheless, I felt like a very lucky toy. *Damn it, I sure know how to get myself into trouble.*

His head moved, his lips inching closer to my ear, to the point where I could feel his hot breath warming the side of my neck. Five more minutes of that, and I was surely going to melt.

Heron was the flame I just couldn't stay away from. And he didn't seem unhappy about that.

"Thank you for letting me sleep here last night," Heron whispered.

My entire body hummed, every inch of me resonating with his voice. It was simply mind blowing, the extent to which my being reacted to him. I nodded slowly, unable to speak. We stayed like that for a while. It felt as though time had stopped. We were fully conscious, aware of each other, our bodies so close and our hearts beating in unison. *Why would I ever want to get away from this?*

His grip tightened, his hands moving slowly and his fingers digging into my flesh. Liquid fire flowed through my veins. My breath hitched, and he reacted, exhaling sharply. I had a feeling that things were about to get a lot more intense, the air thickening around us. I didn't know what to do—the only thing I knew was that I didn't want any of this to stop.

My pulse was racing out of control, and I wondered what would happen if I turned around and just kissed him. My head moved, as if taking executive action on that very thought. Our eyes met, and I nearly lost myself in the twin pools of jade as they seared into me. The tension was almost unbearable, with just an inch between our lips.

I held my breath, hoping that he would do something— that he would read my mind, somehow, and that he would find the courage I seemed to lack. His gaze darkened, temporarily settling on my lips before he pulled himself back and got out of bed.

I blinked several times, unable to wrap my head around the sudden change in the atmosphere. It felt cold now. He looked away and walked over to the door.

"Let's meet downstairs in fifteen minutes," he murmured. "I think we have a long day ahead of us."

Without another word, he left. As soon as I was on my own, everything came crashing down, like a building collapsing in on itself. I broke into a cold sweat, and sat up, rubbing my eyes and trying to figure out what had just happened.

Had I done something? More specifically, had I done something *wrong*?

What had made Heron distance himself so quickly, when nearly seconds earlier we had almost kissed? It made me think that maybe it was better that he hadn't heard me the night before. Perhaps I was better off keeping my feelings to myself, no matter how intense they were getting. He didn't seem interested in following through on whatever this was between us. Or worse, maybe he was afraid. That didn't work out in my favor either, because I had a hard time grasping my own emotions where he was concerned. I certainly wasn't ready to deal with any insecurity coming from him.

At the same time, however, that sudden change in his behavior did warrant a conversation. On one hand, the attraction between us was undeniable at this point. What was still unclear was how we felt about each other, beyond the physical chemistry. His sudden withdrawal made me think that he wasn't as serious about this as I was.

But then again, he didn't know how serious I was... about this.

*Yeah... you need to talk to him.*

# 4

## SCARLETT

### (DAUGHTER OF JERAMIAH & PIPPA)

The clock hadn't struck nine when we all met in the infirmary. Heron and Avril stood idly next to each other, occasionally stealing glances but exchanging not a single word, while we waited for Patrik. Fiona had been kind enough to take care of breakfast, bringing in several flasks of blood, along with some pastries and coffee, the latter mostly for Patrik.

Something had happened between Heron and Avril, but I couldn't put my finger on it just yet. The awkwardness, however, seemed relatively familiar. As soon as I saw Patrik come in and actively avoid looking at me, the familiarity of said awkwardness became more evident. He'd been just as evasive earlier this morning, as well as last night.

I had a feeling that whatever Avril and Heron were going

through, it involved unexpected closeness—the signs were all there, in every sideways glance, in every accidental brush of their hands, and particularly in the rapid heartbeats that were so uncharacteristic of us.

"I've been thinking," Patrik said as he munched on one of the pastries. He gulped down some coffee. "While we're waiting for Harper and the others to come back from the Valley of Screams, we are better off doing some more research about the Imen, while Scarlett and I look for the ingredients I need, to attempt a disruption of the asteroid belt."

"Well, GASP isn't here yet... Not sure *when* they're coming, or *if* they're coming." Fiona sighed. "And this further reinforces my, and I guess *our* suspicion that there is definitely something happening on or around Neraka. Whatever it is, it isn't just preventing us from communicating with our people back home or leaving. I think it's also stopping others from coming in."

"We have until midnight to get as much done about this as we can," Patrik replied, "before Jax and his team come back or, worse, we have to go after them. That gives us a whole day to try and figure out as much as possible. Scarlett and I will go to the Spring Fair. It's a big market day spreading across an entire city level, where they bring in the first of this season's foods. I've learned it's where I can find certain herbs and powders that I'll need to perform a tentative spell aimed at disrupting the asteroid belt. It's a high possibility that the asteroids, which we all know are rumored to have a certain influence on the planet's concealment, can be dispersed with a powerful pulse. It would be like breaking the cycle, disrupting its effect. The only thing is that I'll need your energy to perform this, as it's part of the Druids' dark arts."

We looked at each other for a while, then nodded, silently agreeing that feeling tired and hungry after that spell was performed would be a simple price to pay if it put us in touch with GASP on Calliope.

"That's fine," I replied. "I think it's the least we can do to help you."

"Thank you." Patrik gazed at me softly, a warm flicker in his blue eyes reminding me of our kiss the day before. My chest tightened a little; the memory of his lips on mine made me yearn for more. I was looking at a whole day in his company, and that most likely meant that we would have to talk about what had happened yesterday.

I wasn't sure whether I looked forward to that or not. On one hand, it could lead to a new stage of our relationship—not that what we had was an actual relationship, but it could lead to something new and wonderful. On the other hand, it could lead to him telling me that he was still mourning, that Kyana was still an essential part of him. A pang in my stomach signaled that I would not fare well if the latter came to pass.

"Okay, you guys do that," Fiona said, "and I'll go look for Arrah, because I haven't heard from her yet. I'll go back to the South Bend Inn and see what she's been up to since I returned her brother to her."

"Just be careful, so the other Imen servants don't see you," I replied. "We must remain vigilant and under the assumption that they have all been mind-bent. That may or may not be true, of course, but I think the mindset will keep us sharp."

"I completely agree." Fiona nodded. "I'll be careful. I just need to see her. Arrah has secrets to tell, and now that her brother is safe, and back with her, she's free to tell us everything—whatever that may be."

Fiona then frowned, and exhaled sharply, giving me what seemed like a guilty look. It wasn't like her, and it made me wonder what else she wanted to tell us, but hadn't found the words to yet.

"What's up, Fi?" I asked in a soft voice. "Is there something else you want to tell us?"

"Yeah..." Her shoulders dropped, and she looked at me with wide amber eyes. "I still can't wrap my head around Zane's visit."

Fiona had told Patrik about this last night. Zane coming into the city meant that the protection spell didn't work in keeping the daemons out of Azure Heights. It had prompted Patrik to rush out and alert the Correction Officers, to make sure they stayed vigilant throughout the night. The chances of another attack so soon after the explosions were dim, but existed nonetheless.

"Is there anything else we can do, since the protection spell didn't work?" Avril asked.

"I was thinking about using the swamp witches' cloaking

magic," Patrik replied, "but I don't know whether I will find all the ingredients needed. We will look through the Spring Fair today, and hopefully we'll be able to work something out. Otherwise, we are stuck with being vigilant. I did set some... alarms on the lower levels last night, just to see if any daemons would pass, but none were triggered. It means that they weren't out hunting in the city last night."

"It's worth looking into swamp witch magic," I agreed, then looked at Fiona. "But yeah, it is kind of weird that Zane, the freaking daemon that abducted you in the first place, stopped by to... do what, exactly, say hello?"

"I honestly don't know," Fiona said. "He seems to have a peculiar interest in me. But he didn't mean any harm, even though he kept using those damned yellow powders on me to knock me out whenever I started asking questions. And he kept mentioning that we're not ready for what comes next... though I could not find out what that means, exactly."

"You know," Heron chimed in, "while I do find it alarming that a daemon seems to have the hots for you, I think we could use that in our favor."

Fiona gasped, looking downright alarmed.

"Are you freaking kidding me?" She scoffed. "What the hell do you want me to do? Cozy up to the daemon?"

"What? The guy's obviously interested!" Heron defended his reasoning. "Who knows what kind of influence you could have on him? He could tell you more, eventually, about his people, about their objectives, and about that ominous 'what comes next' part."

A couple of moments went by as we all mulled over Heron's suggestion. The more I thought about it, the less bad an idea it seemed. If Zane was interested in Fiona, and sought to do her no harm, she could definitely try to befriend him. Not only could she get information from him, but maybe she could even persuade him to exert some kind of influence on his people—though that did seem like a stretch for a creature belonging to a nation that thrived on killing innocents and eating their souls.

"Although I'm reluctant," Fiona surrendered, "I might as well take one for the team here."

"Well, that's a double entendre I never thought I'd hear you say," Heron chuckled. Avril immediately slapped him on the shoulder. He rolled his eyes, trying to keep a straight face before a blushing Fiona. "I was kidding, of course. But yes, you could explore this further and see what you could get out of him, as far as the daemons go."

"I must say," Patrik added with a shrug, "I do agree. He may be the enemy, but he did give you back to us, and he even came *here* to see you. It's not often that such a thing happens. It's an interesting anomaly, one you should certainly explore."

"I get it." Fiona sighed. "I'll try a different, friendlier approach the next time I see him. I get the feeling he'll come around again."

"Okay, now that that's out of the way," Avril said, nodding

at Heron, "it's our turn. We saw Hera and Cynara yesterday. We had a brief conversation about the Maras and the Imen, and we can now confirm that there is definitely something weird going on here. Like you said, Scarlett, chances are that more than a handful of Imen have been mind-bent—and for more than just emotional distress, like the Lords claimed. We know the sisters were tampered with, for example, because their memories are faulty, and yet they have knowledge that the Mara people know nothing about. Basically, the Imen are keeping secret archives of their culture, their legends and history. But since the Maras don't know that such archives exist, they have not scraped that knowledge from the Imen's heads."

"The Maras are preventing the Imen from telling us certain things about their lives here," Heron added, "but the Imen's lore seems to have escaped their scrutiny. The sisters directed us to Lemuel, an old Iman who keeps an archive in the slums of level one. We started going through it yesterday, but we'll dig deeper today. We couldn't find anything about the asteroid belt, other than some vague superstitions. Nothing of use, really. But I think our main takeaway is that the mind-bending is far more serious than we originally thought."

"My only question is, where does our diplomacy end?" I asked, looking at Patrik, our senior officer in charge. "Where do we draw the line with what the Maras should and shouldn't do to their people?"

"I'm not sure yet," Patrik replied. "But we obviously can't

trust them. To be specific, we cannot trust the Maras, since they are more manipulative than we thought, and we cannot trust the Imen, since they are the ones who are being manipulated. I don't know how all this relates to the daemons at this point; it could be just an Imen's rights issue, which would make it our business as GASP. But we have to prioritize. The city is under siege from daemons. I say one problem at a time, but stay vigilant nonetheless."

We all nodded, as it was something that we could all agree with. Trust no one. That became our mantra. We only had ourselves to rely on, and maybe Caspian—he came across as different, though still full of secrets.

"Okay, then. I think it's time we all split up, go do our thing, then meet back here in the evening," I concluded, then chugged the rest of my blood.

"Keep your eyes and ears open as you go through the city today," Patrik said as he opened the door. "My traps didn't go off, but given everything else that hasn't worked in terms of magic against the daemons, I suggest we all be more thorough and see if anyone was taken last night. Avril and Heron, you keep digging through Lemuel's archives, and see whatever else you can find out about the daemons, the Maras, and their relationship to the Imen. Fiona, you look for Arrah, and hopefully she'll shed more light on what is going on in this city. We'll see you later."

We went our separate ways. Patrik and I headed up to the Spring Fair, two levels up, which was a more common ground for both Imen and Maras in the city. We didn't say much to each other, and I could feel the tension rising between us with every second that went by. My heart thudded as I tried to think of something to say, while my lips tingled with the need to feel his again.

We had a long day ahead of us—correction: I had a long day ahead of me, as I had to stay close to a Druid who had snuck into my soul, and who I couldn't get out of my head. It was difficult to navigate all this already, given the madness and secrets suffocating this world; having to deal with my feelings for Patrik on top of that made it even more daunting.

# 5

## FIONA

### (DAUGHTER OF BENEDICT & YELENA)

I kept my hood and mask on as I climbed the stairs to the upper level of South Bend Inn, where the Imen servants of the Mara Lords were being hosted until the mansions were rebuilt. The streets buzzed with people, out and about, but there was an overall air of concern and fear lingering wherever I looked.

The inn's ground floor was relatively busy, as the breakfast room was open for the Imen. The smell of pastries and hot coffee tickled my nose. I made my way to the first floor and up to Arrah's room. I knocked on the door, but there was no answer.

I listened for a while, but no sound came from the other side of the door. After a couple more knocks, an Iman from the room next to Arrah's popped his head out, briefly measuring me from head to toe with a curious expression.

"Are you looking for Arrah?" he asked, his voice low, his gaze nervously darting around, as if he didn't want anyone to hear him.

"Yes." I nodded. "Have you seen her?"

He shook his head, then inched closer to whisper.

"Nobody knows where she went," he breathed, "and I don't know when she's coming back, either. But I saw her last night, at around eight, during dinner downstairs. She filled her plate with a lot of food, much more than she would normally eat. She's a tiny little thing compared to the rest of us, so I found it weird that she was packing so much food, which she took upstairs to her room. She didn't even sit down to eat with us."

I figured she had been bringing food upstairs for her brother, Demios, who couldn't be seen anywhere in public, given that I had just broken him out of jail for her.

"Did she say anything? Did she seem... different?" I asked.

"She did seem on edge, maybe a little impatient while she was lining up for the bread." He scratched his head, narrowing his eyes as he remembered. "We only said hello to each other, and I haven't seen her since. Even this morning at breakfast, no one had seen her."

"Thank you," I said, then went back downstairs and outside.

I looked around, carefully analyzing the expression of every Iman coming in or out of the inn. They all looked wary and tired, but none looked at me in a fearful way. If anything, I caught glimpses of hope, as if I was one of the few creatures they wanted to trust.

I, on the other hand, was beginning to feel a little angry and downright disappointed. It seemed as though Arrah had simply disappeared, without a trace, without telling anyone where she'd gone. Most importantly, although I had reunited her with her brother, she'd left without keeping her promise. I could potentially ask Avril to help track her down, but there was still a part of me that was hoping Arrah would come back to tell me more about what she had seen and heard of the Maras, particularly where their treatment of the Imen was concerned.

Avril and Heron were busy with their research for the next few hours, at least, so I figured my time could be put to better use if I checked in on the first level. If Arrah had indeed decided to just disappear, rather than risk her life and her brother's by helping GASP, there wasn't much I could do about it at this point.

The top level of Azure Heights was riddled with construction workers and cleaners, as the reconstruction of the Five Lords' mansions was underway. Piles of rubble and charred wood were being loaded onto large carts, and the Imen cleared the last remnants of the Lords' former residences away, while the construction workers unloaded massive white marble bricks and mounted them over the foundations. With every hour that went by, another foot of wall was built, another sliver of the horrific attack removed and replaced with pristine white stone.

The Lords themselves were moving around, discussing plans with architects and making sure that their preferences and requests were taken into account as the Imen went on building. Vincent was in charge of overseeing the entire reconstruction process, going over plans with the foreman. Emilian, Farrah, and Rowan were discussing city business, from what I could hear—security measures, the Spring Fair, and the general state of the public after the explosions.

Rewa was really coming into her own as Lady of Azure Heights. Two Imen maids followed her around as she circled all five properties and passed out orders to various workers, telling them to look out for a certain gap, or clean up some corner, or do a better job polishing the marble bricks before laying them into walls.

I went up to Vincent and gave them a polite smile as I said hello. He glanced up from his plans and beamed at me, his pale green eyes twinkling.

"Fiona! What a pleasure to see you this morning," he said, then nodded at the foreman to move away and give us some privacy. He moved closer, enough for me to feel slightly uncomfortable, but I was unwilling to show it. Given everything that we had learned over the past day alone, I couldn't have him or anyone else thinking that they were suspected of further wrongdoings.

"I see you are hard at work here." I pointed at the

mansions, all of which had ground-floor walls fully erected, as stairs were being built.

"Yes, well, since the incident two nights ago, my mother decided that I could be given a more active role in rebuilding our homes. She trusts my good taste and architectural instinct." He smiled, pride oozing from his voice.

"Yeah, and I see Rewa is passing out her fair share of orders as well," I replied, watching her as she disappeared behind one of the mansions, along with her maids. Vincent chuckled slightly, then ran a hand through his ginger hair.

"There's only one thing she can do better than any of us— that is, give orders," he said. Sadness darkened his features. "It's also the only thing she can do since her father died. I guess it's her way of coping with the loss of him."

"She strikes me as a very strong young Mara." I sighed. "I imagine she will pull through just fine, and that she will be more than capable of taking his place at the helm of the city, along with your mother and the other Lords."

"I'm glad we agree on that." Vincent smiled softly. "I really enjoyed our dinner last night, by the way, and completely unrelated... I was hoping we could do it again sometime soon."

He changed the subject so quickly that it took me a minute or so to catch up, during which time he simply looked at me, almost adoringly. An uneasy feeling crept up my throat. I gave him a weak smile and thought of good excuses to give him.

Fortunately, Emilian spared me the trouble.

"Fiona! Good to see you! How is everything? Have you

heard from Miss Hellswan and the rest of her team, by any chance? Have they come back yet?" he asked as he walked up to us.

"Lord Obara, good to see you too," I said, thankful that he had cut in. "I will have more information for you by nightfall when the team comes back, provided that we don't have to put together a search party..."

"I must say, I'm very curious as to what they will discover down there," Emilian muttered, scratching his beard. "Before you and your marvelous people got here, we didn't even know what our worst nightmare looked like. So, for that alone, I must thank you once more, on behalf of all of us. I know we're not easy people to deal with, but rest assured we only mean well, even when we seem difficult."

"Thank you, Lord Obara," I replied with a courteous nod. "I stand by our promise to get to the bottom of this, and to find a way to keep your people safe from the daemons. I'm hoping that Harper and the others come back with valuable information. Obviously, the more we know about the enemy, the easier it will be to crush them."

I glanced around for a couple of seconds, noticing the flat stares that Farrah and Rowan were giving me—virtually unreadable. Vincent, on the other hand, was all soft and smiling at me. Zane's warning from the previous night came back to haunt me, adding more turbulence to my stomach. I couldn't help but take his words into account as I looked at

Vincent, and got the distinctive feeling that not all was what it seemed, not even with him.

"I haven't heard of any abductions last night," Emilian said. "Does that mean that the protection spell worked?"

"Unfortunately, no." I sighed. "The spell doesn't work, but we cannot identify the reason. The best we can do is stay vigilant. Patrik added some traps on the lower levels, and he will know if they're triggered. In the meantime, we've asked the Correction Officers to keep a lookout, particularly on the second and third levels of the city."

Emilian didn't seem happy with the notion of daemons still able to simply stroll through the city, but it was the best we could do given the circumstances. He was, by far, the hardest to read, especially considering the Maras' ability to deceive. He came across as the typical all-around good guy, with plenty of wisdom and kindness to pass around, and yet, given what we had learned about mind-bending, I had to admit that not even Emilian could be fully trusted.

It made me feel weird, standing there, surrounded by all these Maras with seemingly good intentions. I knew for a fact that they had systematically wiped the memories of the Imen living in the city. No matter the angle from which I approached this, it did not look good for them.

I couldn't even understand why they were doing it. What were they hiding? What was it that the Imen could not be trusted with, in terms of knowledge about the Exiled Maras? The more time I spent in their presence, the weirder it felt, as if secrets were pushing through the thin and iridescent membrane of reality—*their* reality, to be specific.

As if, any moment now, it would all split open, and all the answers—especially the unpleasant ones—would come pouring out. My only hope was that the truth would come out sooner rather than later, mainly because I had no intention of spending the rest of my life on this wretched planet.

# 6

## AVRIL

### (DAUGHTER OF LUCAS & MARION)

Heron and I went back to Lemuel's studio, deep in the slums of level one. We skillfully broke in, without anyone seeing us. We found the secret switch in his library and gained access to his archives. We barely said a word to each other as we rummaged through the old papers, scrolls, and leather-bound books, looking for anything of use regarding the Imen, the Maras, the daemons, and the asteroid belt.

The Imen's lore was fascinating, I realized as I flipped through the yellowed pages. They were an ancient civilization, with at least fifteen thousand years of existence on this planet. And yet, the ones living in Azure Heights had been reduced to mindless pawns, their memories wiped and their history tucked away in hidden compartments of old walls.

Their mythology was quite interesting, as they worshiped six main deities—the three suns and the three moons. The first and main sun was Kol, the big star around which all seven planets of this system orbited. Kol was the god of light and life. Drul and Khai were, as per the Mara legends, twins of great importance, and the two smaller stars that orbited the sun. From afar, and when the sky was covered in a thin sheet of clouds, it looked as though Neraka had three suns. On any other day, however, the light they shone together was so bright that it looked as though only one large sun stood in the sky. According to the Imen, however, Drul and Khai were the sons of Kol—each entrusted with the power of wind and nature— and not the warriors they were in Mara culture.

The three moons, named Pell, Xus, and Llaim, were the three goddesses. They reigned over the night, and played a crucial role in the wellbeing of this world. However, when brought together, these three goddesses wreaked havoc and "made everything float when they were perfectly aligned with each other". That was a reference to the peculiar phenomenon that Rewa had mentioned when we first arrived on Neraka, in which the three moons were aligned in the sky, in a perfect line, and disrupted Neraka's gravity to the point where anything that wasn't rooted to the ground was lifted, and drifted away until the moons broke rank.

"There's some stuff here about the western tribes," Heron muttered as he browsed through a series of papers. I looked up at him from the chair I had settled into.

"Well, don't keep me on the edge of my seat here."

"Check this out," he said, then read out loud. "'Our people were faced with a choice when the Mara nation prevailed over Azure Heights. We could stay, or we could go. The few of us loyal to the Mara Lords chose to live here, with them. The others, thousands of them, chose a so-called freedom beyond the Valley of Screams, where they settled in the Plains and forests that unraveled miles away, to the west of the gorges.'"

Several seconds went by as I processed the information.

"That's nothing new." I shrugged.

"True, but the next part definitely is," Heron replied, and continued reading out loud. "'The Westerners left us behind, blaming the Maras for their role in the slumber before death, the illness that had taken over our people, claiming those with over four decades in this world. They believed that the Mara nation was to blame. We never took them seriously, and feared that the slumber before death was sent to us by Pell, Xus, and Llaim, for our choice to stay behind. Nevertheless, we couldn't bring ourselves to leave, even when the disease claimed our parents and friends.'"

I raised an eyebrow, leaning into the back of my chair, and exhaled.

"Okay, that is new," I replied. "It sounds as though they were quite the masochists, in a way. I mean, if they thought that their gods were punishing them for staying here, why didn't they leave with the others?"

"Well, knowing the Maras, when the Imen say that they

couldn't bring themselves to leave, to me it sounds as though the Maras... convinced them to stay, if you catch my drift." Heron smirked.

"So let me get this straight. The Imen had the freedom to leave Azure Heights thousands of years ago, but were mind-bent into staying?"

"Most likely. Discreetly. I think that the Maras didn't want *all* of their servants to leave, so they *convinced* a few to stick around, despite the weird disease that kept killing them after their forties." Heron scratched the back of his neck, turning the page. "I mean, this is the stuff of legends, old stories... These people feared the moons, basically, and blamed them for the disease. So I'm not sure how much of this is accurate, but the fact that the Imen from the west suspected the Maras of inflicting 'slumber before death' does ring an alarm bell."

"But how would they do that? I mean, we haven't really looked into the symptoms of this disease." I frowned, trying to find the connection between the Eritopian vampires and the illness. "Do we even know how it manifests? Could it be that, maybe, they're draining their blood? Could blood loss lead to an early death?"

"It's possible, but I haven't seen any bite marks on the Imen, although we both know that they could very well be drinking their blood from other, less visible body parts."

"I think we need to look into this a little more before we jump to any conclusions. All we have to go on, right now, is an ancient manuscript from some Iman from thousands of years ago," I concluded, while my head buzzed with a variety of possible scenarios—none of which were in favor of the Maras.

It seemed as though no matter where we went, or who we asked, or what we read, the story of Azure Heights didn't depict the Maras as the picture-perfect Eritopian vampires they'd initially seemed. This flimsy façade, with beautiful fashion and stunning decor, was exactly that... a façade.

I couldn't help but wonder how much Caspian knew. Unfortunately, he was still out with Harper, so I couldn't exactly just walk up to him and ask. Nevertheless, I did look forward to seeing him again. He was our only way of peeking beyond the curtain, of seeing into the real Azure Heights, the real Maras.

"Whatever this disease is, it's crippling the Imen population. From what I can read here, no one knows what causes the illness, but everyone agrees that it is exclusive to those living in the city. While there are a few elders still, the city's Imen population is dwindling, and most of them don't make it past the age of forty. There's nothing else here about the western tribes," Heron added, "and I get the—"

A thud outside startled us, and we both put our books aside and went over to the window. An Iman had collapsed on the cobblestone in front of the building. His skin was pale, there were dark circles around his eyes, and beads of sweat covered his face. Other Imen gathered around him in a panic.

Heron and I left the studio, then raced down the stairs and outside, to check on the sick Iman. Heron politely pushed the people away, making room for me to kneel down and check the Iman's vitals. I found his pulse, but it was weak and uneven. His heartbeat was slow, and he was running a temperature.

"Does anybody know what happened?" I asked, looking around at the concerned Imen. They all shook their heads and shrugged.

"He just fell," one of them said.

"It's the slumber before death for sure," another chimed in from the back. The others nodded in agreement.

"Has he been sick for long?" I inquired, touching the Iman's face.

"Out of the way," a Correction Officer barked as he pushed the crowd away. He was joined by two others, and all three scowled at us, as if they didn't think we were supposed to be here. It irked me, and I had a feeling that they were here for the Iman. However, I wasn't ready to let go just yet.

"What are you doing here?" I asked, while the Imen moved back, visibly fearful of the Maras with blue insignia on their arms. The first Correction Officer raised an eyebrow at me.

"I could ask you the same thing, milady," he retorted, then looked down at the Iman. "He needs help. We're taking him to the infirmary."

"I've got this," I replied, nervous about letting the Maras take the Iman away. After everything I had just read, I had a hard time trusting these Correction Officers, or anyone else in the city.

"You don't, because you don't even know what *this* is," the Correction Officer shot back.

"She said she's got it," Heron interjected, stepping forward and standing next to me in a protective stance. While I found his gesture endearing, I didn't want him, or us, for that matter, to get in any trouble. All we had were suspicions and nothing else. As much as I hated it, I had to let them take the Iman away.

"It's okay, Heron," I said, then stood and put my hand on his arm, squeezing gently. "He's right, there's nothing I can do. I'm sure the Iman is better off in the care of nurses, upstairs at the infirmary. We can just go check on him later, if anything."

I glowered at the Correction Officer, then moved back, allowing him and his colleagues to lift the Iman off the ground and carry him up to the second level. We watched quietly as they disappeared above, unable to shake the wariness off.

"He isn't the first, nor the last, to just fall like that," one of the Imen said.

Heron and I turned around to face the thinning crowd, as those most wary of the Correction Officers were already walking away. I focused on the young Iman who had just spoken. He seemed to be in his early twenties, and was wearing a waiter's uniform.

"Did you see him collapse?" I asked.

"I only heard the thud." He shook his head. "Then I turned around, and I saw him lying on the ground."

"Do you know him?" Heron replied.

"No, sir, but he had just come out of the perfume store," the young Iman said, pointing at the building next to Lemuel's studio. It was a small building with a white façade, dark brown trim around the windows, and flowerpots cluttered by the entrance. Stylized perfume bottles were drawn on a wooden board just above the door, along with the shop's name: Marion Scents. "I only caught a glimpse of him, as I was on my way to work, before I heard him collapse."

A beautiful, well-dressed Mara stood in the doorway, his shoulder leaning against the frame. He crossed his arms and quietly watched us. His long brown hair was pulled into a ponytail at the back, and his white shirt was rich with dainty ruffles, contrasting the straight lines of his black waistcoat. There were very few Mara businesses that I knew of in these parts of the city—and his was one of them, catering mostly to the Imen.

Heron and I nodded at the Iman, then walked over to the Mara, as the rest of the crowd dispersed. The Mara straightened his back as we reached him. The frown on his face told me that he wasn't fond of speaking to strangers, especially strangers from another world.

"What did you see?" Heron asked him, while I inched a little closer so I could catch a whiff of his scent—his natural scent, to be precise.

"Not much," the Mara replied, his gaze dark and full of secrets he didn't wish to share. He reeked of distrust, among other things. The upside in my ability to sniff out various chemical changes in any living creature was that I had learned to interpret them as emotional reactions, and my accuracy was nearly flawless. "He was just looking around. I think he wanted to buy a perfume for someone, but he didn't. He just walked out and collapsed."

"Was there anyone else inside the store?" I took a step forward, leaving only a few inches between us, and I caught a subtle, lemony note in his sweat. He moved back, uncomfortable with my proximity.

"I don't remember." The Mara shrugged, narrowing his eyes at me. "Are you implying something?"

"What could she be implying?" Heron replied, his jade gaze firm and cold. A muscle twitched in his jaw, and I could feel the tension in the air. One sudden move, and I had a feeling that the Mara would end up against the wall, with Heron's blade at his throat.

The Mara gave us a weak smile, then shrugged, feigning nonchalance.

"Nothing, my lord," he muttered. "I'm just saying, he didn't show any signs of being sick. He was just looking at perfumes, then walked out. Now, if you'll excuse me, I have some business to attend to inside."

He didn't give us a chance to reply. He just turned around and retreated inside his store. We could have gone in, but he definitely wasn't going to tell us more, and we had nothing on him, other than my scent-based assessments.

Heron and I looked at each other for a few moments,

before he took a deep breath and walked over to where the Iman had collapsed. I followed, quietly, watching as he gazed around. He was thinking about something, judging by the way his eyes darted from one spot to another.

"What's on your mind?" I asked him, my voice low.

"I think he's lying," he murmured.

"I can tell you for a fact that he was lying," I said. "His scent was sharp, almost acidic with deceit. Something did happen inside, but I don't think we'll get anything out of this guy, even with force."

"What do you think happened?"

"I don't know. But it probably does have something to do with his condition. I am starting to think that maybe all the lore we've been reading yields more truth than fiction." I sighed. "Maybe the Maras have something to do with this... slumber before death. Maybe they *are* responsible."

"You're right, though, that we won't get anything out of the Mara," Heron replied, running a hand through his short black hair. "But we could ask the Iman."

"Yeah, let's go check on him at the infirmary later tonight." I nodded. "It's best if we let the nurses look after him, for now, and catch him alone if we want to efficiently interrogate him. I doubt he would tell us anything with others around. Then again, they could mind-bend him into silence, but it's still worth a shot."

"That sounds like a plan. Let's get back inside." He walked back into the building housing Lemuel's studio. I followed, although I couldn't stop thinking about the scene we had just witnessed.

The Maras had seen us there, so chances were that they wouldn't try anything against the Iman they had just taken to the infirmary. After all, I did specify that we would go see him later. They knew we'd be coming.

In the meantime, however, we had more research to do. A part of me was anxious about being alone in the same room with Heron again. We hadn't talked about last night. And we'd exchanged barely a handful of words in the morning, after he'd left my room.

I knew I had to talk to him about it, about us—if there even was an *us*. While we were out in the open, I could breathe a little easier, but whenever we were together between four walls, the air condensed, applying a painful pressure on my chest.

He had distanced himself so quickly this morning, I wasn't sure what to make of it. He'd been the one to climb into bed with me, to take me in his arms and hold me tight, his hot breath tickling my ear. He'd been the one to pull me closer when I wanted to move, his touch setting me on fire. And yet, as soon as I had turned to face him, and... maybe kiss him... he darted away, the door closing behind him before I could even realize what had just happened.

I had a feeling that the longer I put off talking to him, the more uncomfortable I would feel. Most importantly, his scent was still toying with my senses, sparking thoughts I'd never had before, about anyone. I shook my head. We walked into the studio, and I locked the door behind us.

But my courage was ragged—in pieces, even, after last night. I'd already said everything I needed to say, but Heron hadn't heard it. I'd figured it would be easier the second time around. But I was wrong... It was twice as hard.

## 7

# HARPER

## (DAUGHTER OF HAZEL & TEJUS)

We went over all possible scenarios, each aimed at getting Caia and Blaze out of Shaytan's palace. From what we had seen up to this point, the royal residence was riddled with guards—daemons the size of wardrobes, massive and bulky, eager to either ram their swords through us, or worse, eat our souls.

All the daemons living in the city were just as ruthless, regardless of their size or service level. We were breakfast, lunch, and dinner for these creatures. Our chances of success were slim, but we were happy even with that sliver of a possibility, rather than staring the impossible in the face. Although, to be honest, I didn't give a damn about chances. All I could think of was getting Caia and Blaze out of there. We needed our fire. I needed my friends back.

"The first thing we need to do is get our hands on some invisibility paste," Caspian concluded, after about half an hour's worth of planning. "Once we vanish, we can get closer to the palace. I saw a smaller tower atop a building near the square. We could use it to scope out Shaytan's residence, the daemons' whereabouts, and, most importantly, Caia and Blaze's position."

"I can use my True Sight to give the place a proper scan, once we get close enough." I nodded in agreement. "We can then draw out a detailed plan on how we infiltrate and extract them."

"We need to have an exit strategy as well. Ideally a plan A and a plan B," Hansa replied, pulling her long, curly black hair back into a ponytail. Whenever she tied her hair up, it meant things were about to get super rough. I'd rarely seen her in such a determined state—it was fearsome and impressive at the same time. "There will be no room for mistakes. We'll have to take every possibility into consideration, including the less... pleasant scenarios."

"What do you mean?" I frowned slightly, using a stick to poke through the ashes in the firepit. We were going to use all of them. Mose had taught us that ashes could mask our natural scents, helping us blend in a little easier with the daemon crowds, without getting sniffed out as foreigners... or midnight snacks.

"We have to be realistic, Harper," Jax interjected, glancing briefly at Hansa, as if he knew exactly what she meant. I looked at Caspian, and he seemed to be on the same page, whereas I felt I was still on the outside, looking in. "We have to assume we might not be able to rescue them. We need to know what we'll do, should we fail."

"Nope." I shook my head and got up, my nerves already frayed as I started pacing through Mose's hut. "I reject that premise altogether. No. We *will* get them out. We *will* succeed. We can't leave room for such doubts. Those thoughts are bound to lead to failure, and I am not walking out of this wretched city without Caia and Blaze!"

"Harper, I'm not saying we won't save them." Hansa stood and came up to me, putting her hands on my shoulders. "We will do our best and more. But I had to bring this up so that we're all on the same page. There are few of us already, and we have to take that possibility into account so we don't lose more of our own in there. Just... Just promise me you'll keep that in mind. It's better to be prepared, that's all. Should we fail, we will have to regroup and try again. But bear in mind, I am not leaving you behind in there."

"We either do this the smart way or we don't do it at all, Harper," Jax replied, giving me a stern look. "I've been through this before. Your sister has been through this, too. Hell, Caia's sister was once a prisoner of the enemy as well. I'm willing to bet that our little fire fae is currently thinking about this, just like we are. This is war. The daemons are the enemy, and they have two of our most precious people. We are going in there to win, to get Caia and Blaze back. But we have to look at it from all possible angles. Should we fail, we must retreat, regroup, and focus on bringing GASP over here to help."

A couple of moments went by. I tried to get my breathing under control. Everything they said made perfect sense, as much as I hated it. I'd been trained for this. I knew what lay ahead. The possibility of failure was real, and no matter how stubborn I was, I couldn't deny it.

"Fine, but we can't exactly rely on GASP now, can we? We only have ourselves," I muttered, then let out a long, almost painful sigh.

"That is correct. For the time being, anyway," Hansa replied. "Baby steps, for now. Let's get our fire fae and dragon out first, then focus on the rest. I just need to know I can count on you to have my back and come out with us, if we're forced to retreat without Blaze and Caia."

I nodded slowly, finding it hard to speak. A knot formed in my throat at the thought of leaving them behind. I knew I wouldn't, but still, it hurt. The mere thought of leaving my friends with Shaytan, the king of daemons—it tore me apart on the inside. My resolve was stronger, though. I chose to focus on freeing them.

*We'll cross that bridge when we get there...*

"What do we do after we get them out?" I asked.

"We head out to the western plains," Jax said. "At least one of us will head back to Azure Heights, to warn the others of what we've seen and learned, while we seek out the rogue Imen. They must have the answers we seek. We might even get them on our side, forge some kind of alliance and rally our forces against the daemons, until we figure out what's keeping us from reaching out to Calliope."

"In that case, I know exactly how we're going to do this," Caspian replied, then grabbed some ragged cloaks off the floor and passed them out. "I know where to go for hunter daemons. They'll have invisibility paste with them. There's an access tunnel not far from here. They use it to deploy to the surface. We can catch them there, then head to the tower near the square. Provided we make our way out through the south-western side of the palace, we can reach the surface through one of the tunnels there. At least two of them lead directly into the western plains."

"I still can't wrap my head around how much you really know about this place," I muttered, irritated.

"Trust me, I wish I could tell you more," he grumbled, looking away as he put a cloak around his shoulders and scooped a handful of ashes from the firepit.

"We will have to talk about this later, Lord Kifo," Jax said, fastening his cloak under his chin. Hansa rubbed ashes over him from head to toe.

Once we were ready to venture through the daemon city, we snuck out of Mose's hut and followed Caspian through a series of narrow alleys and side streets, keeping to the so-called slums, where the weaker, elder daemons lived.

We kept our heads down and covered as we slipped farther east, where crates and barrels were stacked into thick walls, against uneven sets of carved steps leading to several exit tunnels—round, dark holes beckoning us to escape, to run out and never look back. *Not until I get what I came here for.*

"This way," Caspian whispered.

He dashed behind one of the barrel-and-crate faux walls, pointing at the staircase above. I joined him, followed closely by Hansa and Jax. We avoided eye contact with the daemons around us—most of them seemed absentminded, staring blankly at the dirty ground beneath their bare feet as they shuffled up and down the roads snaking into the slums.

They all seemed tired and worn out, with little to no interest in their surroundings. It was as if they were practically braindead, but their bodies, though brittle and old, could still move enough to get them from one place to another, despite having no specific purpose.

"They're reaching the end of their lives," Caspian explained briefly, following my gaze. "They've seen thousands of years in this world. Their bodies can't keep up anymore. Time doesn't forgive the daemons, especially once they stop feeding on souls. Most of them age faster once they stop, if they can't afford to increase their meat intake to counteract the effects. So, they just... wither away, like old trees."

"This is where they come to die, then?" I asked, while Hansa and Jax kept a lookout, checking the stairs above.

"Sort of, yes," Caspian replied. "They lose direction after a while. They just wander around, aimlessly, with nothing to do. Most of them were hunters, spending most of their lives on the surface, roaming freely through the gorges. Once they can no longer provide for themselves, given their old age, they wind up in the care of the kingdom. And as Mose mentioned, the kingdom doesn't care if you're old. It only cares if you can provide for yourself and your people."

"Coast is clear. The crates are filled with something, they're stable to climb," Jax breathed. He gently pushed one of the crates, then climbed up until he reached the stairs.

Hansa, Caspian, and I swiftly joined him, careful not to be seen or heard. We then made our way up to one of the exit tunnels, hiding behind a couple of the broken crates on either side of the opening. Someone was bound to come up sooner or later. All we had to do was jump them.

It didn't take long for two hunter daemons to come along. They were dressed just like the one we'd taken down to the infirmary in Azure Heights, with wide leather belts, off-white loincloths, and various small leather bags hung around their waists, along with thin, curved knives mounted in ivory scabbards on their backs.

Jax took one, and I handled the other. We gripped our swords as we snuck up on them, then slit their throats. Crimson blood gushed out, the daemons falling to their knees. They choked and gurgled until they gave their last breaths. We removed a total of four satchels of invisibility paste, and then Hansa and Caspian dragged them away and hid their bodies behind nearby rocks.

"How long do you think these will last us?" Jax asked, weighing two satchels in his hand as he looked at Caspian.

"I estimate about three to six hours each," Caspian replied.

"We should get more, for Caia and Blaze, too," I murmured. "Besides, we could use some extra for ourselves, and I don't mind killing more of these bastards for it."

A brief smile flickered over Caspian's face. He nodded, and we resumed our positions behind the crates. Not ten minutes later, three more daemons came up. They stopped at the top of the stairs, noticing the dried-up blood on the ground, right in front of the tunnel opening. One of them frowned, letting out a low growl, and sniffed the air.

"I think our non-Nerakian friends were here," he muttered, his red eyes darting around.

I noticed the air rippling behind them, before his partners' throats were split open. Jax and Hansa had already used some of the invisibility paste. The daemon didn't stand a chance, with the other two already down. I jumped out from behind the crate and dashed over to him, thrusting my swords right through his neck.

He stared at me in disbelief, his eyes bulging, as he choked from the two blades cutting through his trachea. Blood poured from his mouth and wounds, glazing his chin and chest. He dropped to his knees. I pushed him down with my foot, pulling my blades out, and Caspian collected six more satchels from him and his dead partners.

We then disposed of their bodies, piling them on top of

each other behind the rocks. Caspian and I swallowed the contents of two satchels, putting the remaining six away. We watched each other disappear in faint, colorful shimmers, until all we could see were delicate ripples through the air whenever we moved.

I caught glimpses of his jade eyes when he looked directly at me. It dawned on me then that this was definitely the result of a difference in using Nerakian ingredients for this particular swamp witch spell.

"The invisibility spell looks different," Jax replied from my right. "It's not as powerful as the original one. I mean, we sort of knew that already from what we've seen of the hunter daemons, but it's interesting to witness it on ourselves. It basically confirms it."

"If you look at me directly," Hansa said, "I can even see your eyes. I think we have to be careful about where we look, once we get back in there. Avoid eye contact with anyone at all times."

"We should also agree on some kind of sound signal, so we can identify where we are in proximity to each other," Caspian replied. "We can't exactly hold hands all the time. Perhaps a triple whistle?"

Hansa gave out three short whistles, clear enough to be heard, but not loud enough to be overheard past a twenty to thirty-yard radius. I responded with a similar set of sounds, which Jax and Caspian returned.

"Okay, we're good to go," Caspian said. "We'll go back

down the way we came, then take the main belt road to the north, past the slums. Let's regroup at the red tower outside the main square."

"I think, for safety's sake, we should split into pairs until we get there," Jax replied. "I'll take Hansa, and you take Harper, Lord Kifo."

"Agreed," Caspian breathed, then found my hand, wrapping his long fingers around it and squeezing gently. "Let's move."

I realized then just how aware of my presence Caspian was. He paid attention, in our invisible form, to my breathing and low heartbeat. He most likely followed my scent, too, thus knowing exactly where I stood at all times. It was perfectly reasonable for us to use our other senses when we couldn't see each other.

Caspian and I rushed down the stairs, making our way back into the city. Hansa and Jax were not far away, and we all advanced up the main belt road toward the north side. We'd made this trip before, when we'd first gotten into the city.

Once we reached the neighborhood housing Mose's hut, we made a sharp turn left and followed the sinuous and narrow roads into the city center. I could see the palace and its majestic tower rising in the distance. Not far from it was a smaller red tower where we were due to rendezvous. It was also going to be my vantage point, from where I would use my True Sight to scan the area and find Caia and Blaze.

It was an easier trek through the city of daemons when

they couldn't see us. I could breathe better, even though we were surrounded by bloodthirsty enemies. And to think, just a couple of months earlier, I'd been dropping hints to Derek and my dad that I wanted to score a field mission. For a brief moment, I wondered if I would've been better off going to Tenebris and dealing with the incubi rebellion instead.

The warmth of Caspian's hold spread through my arm, raising my temperature as we darted through the streets. *No, there is nowhere else I'd rather be.*

Our predicament was far from pleasant. Our lives were at risk, our friends were prisoners, and our families were millions of lightyears away. And yet, with Caspian so close to me, I had to admit... I was right where I needed to be.

## 8

HANSA

We kept an eye out for red garnet lenses, as there were plenty of daemons throughout the city who could be using them. We stayed in the shadows, waiting for larger groups to pass by before we went back into the streets, on our way to Shaytan's palace.

The rowdy crowds that we'd seen earlier, during the general assembly, had scattered, with just soldiers left patrolling the alleys, and the occasional civilian. Amber fires burned at junction corners and in wall-mounted iron sconces, casting an orange light over the black stone and obsidian structures.

Half an hour later, we reached the main square. On the right side, facing the wide-open space, was a large rectangular building made entirely from black bricks, with a six-story tower that had been painted in deep shades of red.

Jax and I waited outside, by the northeastern corner, the closest to the entrance. I scanned the area around us, looking for signs of air rippling, movements that could suggest that Harper and Caspian were close by. I caught a brief glimpse of jade eyes, and I knew that they, too, had made it. I gave out a low triple whistle.

I felt Harper bump into me, making me sigh with relief.

"Good to see we all made it," Caspian whispered.

"We need to make our way up there, into the red tower," I said slowly, keeping an eye out. Several daemons passed by, a combination of males and females in elegant leather attire, with plenty of gold and precious gemstones adorning their necks, chests, and shoulders. They were some kind of nobility, I figured.

There were also soldiers moving up and down the stretches of road framing the main square. I could see red lenses hanging from slim gold chains, and mounted on their belts. At least they didn't have them on at all times.

"We can go through the main entrance," Harper breathed. "I checked—there are barely any daemons for us to worry about. Mostly common workers, and just two guards on the ground floor. We can go all the way to the top."

"Okay then, I'll sort of see you upstairs," I quipped, then made haste toward the main entrance, without letting go of Jax's hand.

We rushed through the wide-open double doors, darting past the two guards that Harper had mentioned, then up the six flights of stairs to the top. I nearly bumped into one of the workers coming down. He was carrying a burlap sack on his shoulder, filled with what I assumed was rubble, judging by the crumbling sound. Jax swiftly pulled me back to the side, holding me as the daemon went about his business.

"Thank you," I whispered, and Jax responded with a tight squeeze of his arms around my waist, his hot breath tickling my face.

"I'll never pass up an opportunity to hold you, no matter what the excuse," he replied, murmuring softly in my ear. He always had this way of setting me on fire with a handful of words, but it was all the more intense now that we were actually together and openly flirting. It warmed me up on the inside, as I knew that he was there for me. Jax was my fuel to keep moving and fighting, slashing my way through an entire city of daemons if it meant emerging alive, with his arms around me.

"And I'll never deny you such an opportunity." I whispered, as we continued our race up the stairs.

I could almost feel him smiling. We took two steps at a time, until we made it to the top. I let out another triple whistle, and Harper responded.

This level was empty, just the smooth floor and several small, round windows carved into the stone, with no glass. I saw the air rippling near one as Harper moved closer so she could use her True Sight and scan the entire palace. She needed a high vantage point to get a better spatial assessment of the building, as seeing through layers of stone and marble from the ground floor didn't do much in the absence of a high angle.

I kept quiet for a few minutes, listening to the noises below. The daemons were hard at work, lugging sacks of rubble from one level farther down to the next, while their foreman barked orders from the first floor. From what I'd seen on my way up, they were renovating two of the upper floors, breaking down several walls in the process.

Had it not been an urgent situation of rescuing Caia and Blaze, I would've taken the time to further observe the daemons at work. They had their customs, their routines and processes, an interesting hierarchy, and a rule of law. If not for their eagerness to eat our souls, they would have been a joy to study, as a foreign people from another world.

Unfortunately, they had decided to snatch two of my people. My diplomacy had flown out the window a long time ago as far as the daemons were concerned. All I could think of were ways of making them pay, of making them suffer for what they had done to us—not to mention the thousands of innocent Maras and Imen.

# 9

## HARPER

### (DAUGHTER OF HAZEL & TEJUS)

I took my time with each wing of the palace. I memorized every hall, every set of stairs, and every corridor, down to the last detail. I made mental notes of the guards' movements, noticing their patterns and routes throughout the palace. Most importantly, I identified two areas of roughly fifty square yards that I could not see through, even with my True Sight.

Shaytan and a couple of his advisers were in the east wing, in his throne room—a superb, enormous space with gilded panels and soft, red velvet curtains covered in gold embroidery and delicate gemstones. Farther down from his throne room, five of the seven princes were chatting around a long, rectangular dinner table, as daemon servants loaded their plates with strips of raw meat. At the end of the table, four Imen were bound to their chairs, watching in horror as their captors talked and laughed over dinner. I had a feeling that the Imen's souls were meant for dessert.

A shudder ran through me, and chills traveled down my spine. I couldn't wait to run the princes' throats through with my swords.

I shifted my focus back to the areas that I couldn't see through. They were basically two large metallic boxes—I assumed they'd been cast from meranium, judging by their polished finish and peculiar shade of gray. Whether it was a charm or something else, I couldn't get past them.

"I think I know where they are," I muttered, then fumbled through my backpack for some chalk. I always kept some with me, in case Patrik needed it for an impromptu spell. "There are two small sections in the palace that I can't see through. I spotted them before, when we were running away from the crowd, but I didn't get a chance to study them properly."

"Could they be charmed in any way? Swamp witch magic, maybe?" Hansa replied.

"Could be," I answered, then got down on my knees and started drawing a rough schematic of the palace, marking all the key areas and possible access routes to the meranium boxes. "This is the main entrance into the palace."

I drew a tiny X on the stylized map, then drew dotted lines to mark two ways in, reaching through both the east and the west wings, before they met in the middle of the south wing.

"I'm guessing you want us to split up?" Jax asked.

"Yes," I replied, circling the locations of the meranium

boxes on both sides, along with a number of X's, representing the guards' positions throughout the palace. "They could either be here... or here. Our best bet is to cover both sides simultaneously. One of us will come out with Caia and Blaze. The king is here, talking to... counselors, I guess. The princes, or at least five of them, are in here, enjoying dinner. They are also about to feast on the souls of four Imen. I would love nothing more than to chop their horned heads off, but Caia and Blaze are our priority."

"I agree," Caspian said, and I heard him moving closer to me. "Harper and I will take the west side, and Jax, you and Hansa should take the east wing."

"There are approximately three hundred yards from the nearest set of stairs to the meranium boxes on both sides," I added, drawing slim lines as I further explained the best routes through Shaytan's palace. "From what I could see, there are plenty of archways, massive sculptures, large decorative objects, and curtains mounted throughout the hallways and corridors, giving us a plethora of hiding places along the way. We can check both meranium boxes simultaneously."

"Which floor? Because that palace is huge," Hansa muttered.

"The second floor. They're both on the second floor, so at least we have that working for us." I sighed. "There was no sign of Blaze and Caia anywhere else. My instinct tells me they are where I cannot see them."

"And what's that thick dot you drilled in the middle of the south wing?" Jax asked.

"Well, since we have no means of communicating with each other," I explained, "I figured we could use this as our meeting spot. It's a huge, floor-to-ceiling totem, made entirely out of gold. Its figures have large, gemstone eyes. You cannot miss it."

"How long do you think this will take us?" Caspian replied.

A couple of moments went by as I waited for Jax or Hansa to give us some estimates, simply wondering if their figures matched mine. I wanted to keep it under an hour, a basic in-and-out operation.

"It could be anything between thirty minutes and four hours," Jax said. "It depends on how smoothly it all goes in there. If we get in with no hurdles, and we get to the meranium boxes, we have to assume that there will be guards inside, along with some sturdy swamp witch magic to deal with, before we can get Blaze and Caia out."

"To be honest," Hansa chimed in, "I would like for us to take some time, at least half an hour to forty-five minutes, to survey the interior of that palace and make some mental notes as to what goes on in there. The more information we can gather on our enemies, while we are in there, the better and easier it will be for us to organize future strikes against Shaytan and his people."

"You make a fair point," I conceded. "As eager as I am to rescue Blaze and Caia, I agree that we should move slowly. Not just for the purpose of observation, but also to be cautious. There are plenty of red lenses in that palace, waiting to nab us."

"Speaking of which," Jax said, "we should definitely get our hands on some of those lenses going forward. We'll have better opportunities for that. We are invisible, and perfectly capable of lifting them off the daemons without physically engaging them."

"Sure thing, Jax. Just don't tell the others that you turned us into pickpockets," I quipped.

Some of the tension around us had already started to dissipate. We had a plan, and we had a clear map of the palace interior. There were plenty of enemies to avoid along the way, but we had what felt like an accurate idea of where our friends were being kept.

It was part of our nature, as GASP agents, to not let any situation bring us down to the point where we couldn't make light of it. As long as we could joke about it, our mindset was positively calibrated for success. The moment I allowed darkness to eat away at me and my resolve was the moment of absolute failure.

*And there is no room for failure in this wretched city.*

# 10

---

## JAX

Harper wiped the map away, leaving no trace of our presence there. Then we split up into pairs again and snuck out of the red tower. We darted across the main square, keeping away from the soldiers, then rushed up the palace stairs and into the enormous obsidian structure.

From the outside, the palace looked huge, stretching for at least a mile on each side. But from the inside, it looked even bigger, with shiny, perfectly polished floors and walls over twenty feet in height. Decorative molding brushed with gold dust framed the ceiling and the bottom part of the walls.

Ghastly sculptures of what I assumed were legendary daemons and various underground creatures, including pit wolves and death claws, lined every corridor with imposing dimensions. They'd been carved out of the same fine obsidian

crystal, and the amber lights of torches and overhead chandeliers cast their reflections against their multifaceted surfaces.

As we made our way into the east wing, I caught glimpses
of adjacent banquet halls. Their walls were embedded with
precious gemstones and gold inlays laid out in intricate works
of art. Heavy furnishings made of black wood filled every
room. Rich, beige leather drapes covered the tall, floor-to-
ceiling windows. In some of the chambers, they'd replaced
leather with red velvet. The ceilings were all painted with
ample scenes of what looked like daemon lore, in vivid colors
with dramatic contrasts.

Sturdy columns with beautifully sculpted crowns held up
the high ceiling, like ancient giants looking down on us from
both sides, as we moved to the spacious hallway. Harper was
right—there were plenty of hiding spots for us, as well as
dozens of daemon soldiers patrolling this part of the palace.

Hansa and I had to get out of sight a couple of times when
guards carrying red lenses passed by. We took our time
advancing through the east wing, as I analyzed the daemons'
weapons and movements. Each of them carried two broad
rapiers, along with round shields on their backs and additional knives mounted on leather belts strapped to their
thighs. Not all of the soldiers carried red lenses, but on aver-
age, one out of three patrolling this part of the palace had one.

"Stay here," Hansa whispered, and I felt her leave my side.

We'd hidden behind a giant death claw statue, its lowered
wings shielding us from a passing trio of daemon soldiers. I

saw the air ripple where she moved, as she snuck behind the grunts and proceeded to lift the red lens off the one in the middle.

I held my breath, watching quietly as the round red garnet disk hovered in the air for a brief second, before it disappeared. One of the daemons made a sudden movement and bumped into her with his elbow. I froze as the daemon frowned and realized that someone was there.

Cursing under my breath, I ran out from our hiding spot and drove my sword through that daemon, while the other two jumped back, trying to figure out what was going on. The soldier in the middle patted his chest, looking for the red lens.

"Looking for something?" Hansa's low voice made them growl, and they moved to attack.

They followed the air ripples, taking their swords out in the process. I pulled mine from the collapsed daemon and proceeded to attack the soldier on the left, while Hansa handled the former owner of the red lens. While we had caught the first one by surprise, the other two were better prepared and much faster than the ones we'd encountered before.

I had a little bit of trouble killing my opponent, but after dodging three of his hits, I managed to thrust my blade through his head from below, careful to move away and not get any blood on me. Hansa grunted, and I watched the third daemon drop to his knees. A wide gash blossomed at the center of his chest as he gave out his last breath and fell flat on his face.

We immediately dragged their bodies away, stuffing them behind the death claw statue against the wall. The blood on the floor was hard to notice at a glance—I took comfort in that as I found Hansa's hand and pulled her away and farther down the hallway.

"It won't take long before someone sees the blood and finds the bodies," I muttered.

"I swear, I tried to be as discreet as possible," Hansa replied, "but the guy moved out of nowhere. Thanks for the help, though. At least we have a red lens now."

"That's good, now we just need to get as far away from that hotspot as possible."

According to our current position, the meranium box was somewhere ahead, about 200 yards away. We kept to the side, sneaking behind statues and decorative curtains, doing our best to stay away from the central part of the hallway, as more daemons patrolled these parts.

The tension that had been brewing between Hansa and me for the past three months had dissipated from the moment we'd kissed in that dirty old basement. As soon as I accepted my fate, and understood that my life was worthless without her, I could see everything clearly again.

Even as we walked through enemy territory, my resolve was stronger than ever. After all my misfortunes in terms of soulmates, I'd actually found hope that it wouldn't end in

tragedy this time around. The synergy between us was undeniable. Hansa was a terrific fighter, and she made me better, too,
just by being there with me.

We'd been made for each other, and I couldn't deny that
any longer. Of course, I'd already promised myself to address
this... whatever this was between us, once we got out of this
city. I didn't know where it was going, but I didn't want to lose
the newfound harmony between us—it helped us work better
together, as if we read each other's minds and knew exactly
what we were going to do.

There would come a point when I'd have to sit down and
talk to her. There was so much about me that she didn't know,
that she had to understand so that she would not hate me for
having been such a coward over the past few months. The
thought of losing her still haunted me, but the thought of her
alive and not in my arms was far worse.

The coast was clear ahead. I took advantage of that sliver of
peace and temporary safety, due to our invisibility, to stop
behind another statue and pull her close to me. I wrapped my
arms around her and lowered my head so I could breathe in
her scent—the ashes we'd rubbed on ourselves had failed to
mask her spicy scent of leather and wild roses.

"Jax, as much as I'd love to, I'm not sure this is the right
time to—"

"I just need a second with you, that's all," I murmured, my
lips brushing against her smooth cheek. "There's so much

about me that you should know, and I plan to make it out of here alive so I can tell you everything."

"If this is about whatever emotional baggage you've been carrying around and using as an excuse to keep me away, then yeah, I look forward to hearing about it," she replied softly.

"Okay, but for the time being, can you just promise me that you will stay by my side and not do anything too crazy, that you will at least talk to me before you pull a Hansa on me?"

"Define 'pulling a Hansa'," she said, gently nuzzling my neck.

She felt so hot in my arms, so soft and perfect. I'd spent a long lifetime feeling incomplete, and the universe had finally rewarded me. The problems, however, did not escape me. I could never perform Pyrope with her, and I had to admit that, deep down, it did make me a little bit sad. Nevertheless, there were plenty of other ways in which I could make her understand exactly how crazy I was about her.

"Running off, charging a horde of daemons like the warrior succubus you are, only for me to jump in and stop at least one of them from decapitating you?" I grinned, my lips looking for hers.

"Keep it up, and you will have more than daemons to worry about." She slowly lifted her head, responding to my search.

"Don't get me wrong, I do enjoy rescuing you," I replied, trying to keep myself steady on my feet. She was reining her succubus nature in, but her effect on me was still close to devastating. "It makes me feel a little less... useless when I'm around you."

"Darling, you are anything but useless to me."

Movement twenty feet away from us made me freeze. We stilled, barely breathing, and watched as two more soldiers passed us by. I held her tight, feeding off her strength while trying to keep a clear head—her body so close to mine left me dazed, barely functional. I exhaled as soon as the soldiers got farther away.

"I look forward to continuing this conversation later," Hansa whispered, then took my hand. We moved farther west toward the meranium box.

I'd stared death and destruction in the face a few too many times over the years. I'd learned to take advantage of every second, of every moment when I could simply stop and enjoy the smallest, most beautiful things in life—and holding Hansa in my arms, feeling her skin on mine, and inhaling her dazzling scent had definitely been worth it.

But it was time to get our "kids" out of here. Just as I'd gotten my chance to show Hansa how I truly felt, Blaze and Caia deserved the same. However, if Blaze didn't take his relationship with Caia to the next level once we got them out, I figured I'd have to smack him over the head in order for him to see what he was missing out on.

Nothing bloomed more beautifully or more powerfully than love at the core of adversity.

# 11

## HARPER

### (DAUGHTER OF HAZEL & TEJUS)

Our journey through the west wing was uneventful for the first hundred yards, as we snuck through the main hallway and got a good feel for our surroundings. The architecture, the predominance of black stone and obsidian, contrasting with the glamorous array of gold and gemstones and the warm light coming down from torches mounted on the walls and heavy gold chandeliers above, created a very imposing setting.

The daemon soldiers patrolled the wing in groups of two to three, with one always carrying a red lens. We stayed on the side, moving behind statues and soft leather curtains, occasionally stopping to allow the daemons to pass. We couldn't risk them even hearing us move.

"Two hundred yards ahead," I whispered.

"The coast looks clear," Caspian breathed, then took my hand as we walked another twenty feet or so, before more soldiers emerged from a nearby hall.

"There are more of them here than what I saw earlier from the red tower," I muttered. Caspian pulled me close to him, behind a statue of a large pit wolf. I could feel his heart beating against my chest, nervously thudding as we waited for the soldiers to go by.

If it weren't for Blaze and Caia stuck somewhere in this palace, I would've gladly stayed here in his arms for much longer—daemons be damned. The red glimmer of a lens caught my eye, and I gently pushed myself away from him.

"Don't move," Caspian whispered.

"We need a lens," I replied, my voice barely audible.

I didn't give him time to protest or hold me back. Light on my feet, I dashed behind the soldiers and discreetly reached out and lifted the red lens off the daemon in the middle. He didn't feel it, not even when I used my index finger and thumb to unclasp the little metal ring holding the chain attached to his belt.

They kept walking, and I moved along with them, until I retrieved the red lens and came to a halt. I watched them go farther down, clearly unaware of my presence. Resisting the urge to pat myself on the back, I turned around to go back to Caspian, but I froze. My heart skipped a beat, plummeting into my stomach. My blood ran cold.

Only thirty yards away from me was Shaytan, accompanied by the two counselors I'd seen earlier. What the hell were they doing in the west wing? I'd figured they'd still be in the east wing, specifically in his throne room, as far away from me as possible.

They were walking toward me, but they had yet to see me, or even notice the air rippling from any movement on my part. I glanced to my right, where I caught a glimpse of Caspian's jade eyes. I could only imagine the look on his face, since I couldn't see it. Although I was pretty sure my face wasn't exactly the textbook definition of "serene" either, at this point.

I shifted slowly to the side, holding my breath as Shaytan and his counselors got closer. The king was visibly aggravated, adding weight to his every word as he barked orders at the two noble daemons.

"You cannot possibly tell me that in the city of daemons, where we sniff out everything and everyone, where we have red garnet and plenty of other artifices, you can't find those wretched outsiders," Shaytan hissed. "I want them found. Yesterday, not today, and not tomorrow."

"My lord, we are doing our best," said one of the counselors, his voice trembling. He wore the same gold thread on his horns, but its woven pattern was simpler, and it didn't cover their full length. He clearly wasn't a prince, but the abundance of jewels around his neck identified him as part of the nobility. "But these outsiders seem to be a lot smarter and more resourceful than we originally thought."

I managed to hide behind another statue, just as the king and his counselors passed by.

"That is not an excuse. You know they'll be coming for their friends," Shaytan replied bluntly. "Make the necessary arrangements. Instruct your guards to keep the red lens on at all times and to look out for any... unexpected visitors. I want them captured, and I want them captured alive."

"Yes... Yes, my lord," the other counselor replied.

Caspian reached me, placing his hand on my shoulder to let me know he was there. Neither of us moved as we continued to eavesdrop on the king, who was walking away.

"It is imperative that we keep them in the city," Shaytan said. "Under no circumstances can they be allowed to return to the surface. We did not make it this far for these little mice to ruin our plans, did we?"

"No, my lord," the first counselor agreed. "You are right, we must mobilize our forces and be extra vigilant until we capture the entire GASP team. I will make sure that the palace guards are aware."

"Good, because I am losing my patience," Shaytan grumbled. "I ache to taste their souls... Their species are all far more powerful and intense than our poor little Imen."

"Speaking of which, my lord, why haven't you tried the ones we already have?" the second counselor asked.

"Soon enough, Rozell, soon enough. Before I get there, I have other plans for them. They'll be staying with us for a while, whether they like it or not," the king replied.

"Father." A fourth voice shot across the hallway from the opposite end. It prompted Shaytan and his counselors to come to a halt and turn around.

This was one of the princes on the council, judging by his gold threaded garb, but I hadn't seen him earlier, during the assembly. By process of elimination, I realized that I was looking at Zane, as he sauntered toward his father. His confident stride was matched by his imposing figure. His leather pants, which hugged his muscular thighs, were tucked into his calf-high boots. His chest was bare, ropes of muscle drawing shadows on his abdomen, and he wore a heavy leather cape on one shoulder, fastened with a solid gold buckle. His long black hair was braided down his back, the ends packed with gold beads, and his horns were adorned with gold thread, just like his brothers'.

However, unlike the other princes, Zane came across as extremely confident, and much less dependent on his father. Somehow, his choice to release Fiona started to feel more like an act of rebellion against Shaytan, rather than anything else. Chances were that the king had no idea about the whole Fiona incident.

"Ah, my wayward son," Shaytan huffed, slowly raising an eyebrow. "Unless you have something useful to say, I have no time for your bleeding-heart nonsense."

"What bleeding-heart nonsense is that, father?" Zane replied, stopping in front of the king and his counselors. "Perhaps you're referring to my repeated warnings about underestimating the outsiders? My plea for you to stop with all this nonsense and act like a king, for once in your life?"

"I am more of a king than my father before me, and I am more of a king than you ever will be," Shaytan shot back, gritting his teeth. His canines protruded menacingly, a sure sign of aggression. Zane clearly had a way of getting on his father's nerves. Shaytan then smirked, his arrogance making my stomach churn. "Then again, chances are you will never be king, anyway."

"Yes, that's fine." Zane rolled his eyes, as if having heard this before, one too many times. "Nevertheless, my warnings ring true, and you know it. Stop chasing the outsiders. Keep your distance, and mind your business. Do not engage them. You haven't seen what I've seen. Do not underestimate them—that is all I am saying."

"My son, I am still baffled by your lack of faith in my ability to not only rule this magnificent kingdom, but also to handle a bunch of unruly outsiders who seem to think they are better than us, and who are sticking their noses where they do not belong."

"They are not to be played with." Zane shook his head. "For how long do you think you'll be able to keep that dragon in his cage? They are fast, and quick learners. Before you know it, they will turn you into ashes, and we all know that our world is not ready for Cayn."

"And you continue to not only insult me, but your brother, too," Shaytan scoffed, looking genuinely disappointed. Clearly

Zane and his father had a bit of a tumultuous relationship, and the king wasn't exactly happy with his youngest. If he knew what I knew, Shaytan would've probably been much angrier at this point.

"I don't wish to insult you, Father, but you are being incredibly stubborn. I keep telling you that I've seen them in action back in the gorge, that I know what they are like, and I am telling you, for the millionth time, that you are in over your head."

"Your Highness," the first counselor replied, his tone gentle, echoing the patience of a parent. "We all understand your concerns, but the king knows what he's doing. He has been leading our people for thousands of years, longer than any monarch before him. There is a reason why he still stands on the throne, and the people both love and fear him. A bunch of outsiders will not get the best of us, and they will certainly not get the best of the king."

I stifled a groan, my fists balled so tightly that my nails were digging into my skin to the point that it hurt, but it was that pain that stopped me from going out there and drawing my swords. It took every ounce of common sense that I could find to hold it together.

Caspian must have felt the tension building up inside me, somehow. I felt him gently squeeze my shoulder, as if reassuring me that he was there, and by my side.

"My son." Shaytan pressed his lips into a thin line as he glowered at Zane. "I would like, at this point, to remind you that you are *not* involved in this, per your choice. In fact, if I catch you meddling with my affairs in this matter, you will be exiled or worse."

"Worse? What is worse than this?" Zane scoffed, crossing his arms over his chest in a defiant stance.

Shaytan didn't say anything for what felt like maybe a minute, but his red eyes spoke volumes in the place of words.

"I have plenty of sons to take your place on the Council," he replied. "And you know what it takes for a prince to be replaced on the Council, don't you, my son?"

"So, what you're saying is that I should not care or get involved in this suicidal master plan of yours, or I will get kicked out, or worse, killed," Zane voiced the conclusion.

"This is the underground, Zane. True Neraka. The real Neraka. The land of daemons. There is no room for sympathy or weakness, and you are displaying both when it comes to those puny outsiders," the king shot back. "Now, be a good boy and go serve your kingdom, like a good son. Make your mother proud and stop getting on my nerves."

Zane watched as his father and his counselors walked away, the king's footsteps heavy on the black marble floor. He shook his head slowly, unable to take his eyes off Shaytan, until he disappeared behind a corner, farther to the south.

I wondered if it would be a good idea to approach him. He clearly didn't get along with his father, but I had no guarantee that he wouldn't turn us in if he saw us. I couldn't rely on an assumption that, if he'd let Fiona go, he was an overall good guy. Like Hansa had said, we were at war.

Zane stood there for a while. Caspian and I waited for him to go anywhere, as long as it was as far away from us as possible. We had a meranium box to get to, less than two hundred yards away. But he didn't move. Instead, he took out his red lens, and turned his head to look directly at us.

For the second time in less than fifteen minutes, I felt my heart stop.

"Oh, crap," I muttered, my hands instinctively reaching for my swords.

"Relax," Zane replied, exhaling. "If I wanted you dead, I would've given you away five minutes ago."

"You mean to tell me you knew we were here?" I asked, sensing the tremor in my voice that was uncharacteristic of me.

"Don't get me wrong," Zane grinned, "the king definitely didn't know you were here, so your covert skills are not too bad, but they're not good enough to fool *me*."

A couple of seconds went by as I went over all our options, given this new development. Would we simply part ways, pretend we never saw each other? Or would I be able to persuade him to help us rescue Blaze and Caia?

"I'm guessing you're here for your friends?" Zane pursed his lips and raised an eyebrow at us.

"Well, at least you're the sharp one out of the bunch," Caspian muttered from behind me. I gave him a subtle nudge with my elbow, enough to stop him from talking. His sarcasm, while at most times refreshing, wasn't going to help us in this moment.

"Have you seen them?" I asked.

"Yes. They're both fine, for the time being. However, they're trapped, and your friend—you know, the big one that spits fire? He can't exactly go dragon. Not without crushing the other one. The feisty one." Zane chuckled lightly.

His description of Blaze and Caia was surprisingly blunt and accurate.

"Can you help us? Can you help us get them out of here?" I crossed my fingers behind my back. Not that I was superstitious in any way, but we sure needed a stroke of luck this time.

"Didn't you just hear my father?" Zane retorted. "He doesn't have a habit of making empty promises."

"Would he really kill you?" I still had a hard time imagining that. Blood is thicker than water, after all.

"Well, I haven't exactly been the model citizen, nor the perfect son." Zane shook his head. "I am easily replaceable. You don't know him like I do."

"But he doesn't even need to know," I insisted. "You can just take us to them. I know there are two meranium boxes in this palace, but I don't know if we are in the right place."

"You're in the right place," he confirmed. "They're over there. A hundred and eighty yards down this hallway."

"Are you afraid of your father?" Caspian interjected.

Zane narrowed his eyes at him, stifling a smirk.

"Haven't you seen the guy? He's huge, and he commands our entire army."

"Listen," I said, "I understand if you're afraid, but how can you possibly live with yourself, if you leave two innocent creatures to get their souls eaten like that? Is that how you people live?"

"Okay, first of all," Zane shot back, taking a couple of steps forward, "your friends are nowhere near innocent. They've killed hundreds of my people. Second, the only person I've ever been happy around has been myself. Leaving you and your insanely reckless clique to rot in this place won't change that."

I raised my hands in a defensive gesture, feigning resignation.

"None of us would ever kill a daemon just for the fun of it. Everything we do is to defend ourselves and those who need protection, those who are vulnerable. All life is precious, and that is what we fight for," I replied. "Everything that Blaze and Caia did was either in self-defense, or to save innocent lives. But, anyway, I understand. You don't want to piss off your dad, and I get that. You're not the rebellious type. It's cool."

I moved to walk away, taking Caspian's hand in mine. It only took about twenty seconds for Zane to let out a frustrated groan, prompting the both of us to stop and turn around to look at him.

"Okay, fine," he said. "I'll help you."

"Thank you," I replied.

"Don't thank me. I'm not doing it for you. You're lucky I'm pissed off with my father and I'd love to ruin his day. Besides, you two have no idea how to bypass the charms on that box," Zane scoffed.

"You won't regret it." I tried to offer something in return, anything—even some kind of assurance. "My team will be made aware that you helped us. Whatever comes after this, I'll make sure you're safe."

"Oh, gee, thanks. I'm already regretting it. But I promised I'd help. I'm a daemon of my word," he said. "Anyway, get moving. Stay close to me and keep quiet. I've got some business to take care of before I can show you to your friends."

"Are you sure we can trust him?" Caspian whispered in my ear, his hot breath knocking me off my focus for a split second.

"You can go ahead by yourselves, if you want to," Zane replied, his hearing as sensitive as I'd imagined. I figured Caspian knew that, too, and had wanted him to hear. "But you're helpless with those charms."

"You heard him," I said, keeping my tone even. "He's a daemon of his word."

With no other choice but to accept that one of Shaytan's sons was on our side, Caspian and I walked over to Zane and assumed positions in his proximity, taking advantage of his broad frame to stay out of sight from other daemons passing by.

Less than a hundred and fifty yards away was a meranium box, and my friends were in it.

I was ready to partner up with whomever I came across, if it helped me get them out of there. Somehow, Zane didn't strike me as such a compromise. I was willing to bet that his daddy issues ran much deeper than what we'd already witnessed.

# 12

## SCARLETT

### (DAUGHTER OF JERAMIAH & PIPPA)

The Spring Fair was an interesting event to explore. Almost half of the city's fourth level had been slightly adjusted to fit dozens of market stalls, the streets lined with warm white lights strung beneath the massive textile awnings that kept the sun out.

Merchants from all over the city had gathered to sell a variety of items, from books, quills, and artisanal inks to works of art, miniature sculptures, perfumes, soaps, fabrics, and jewels, as well as fashionable garments, fine furs, tools and instruments, and plenty of local food and drinks.

It was truly a pleasure to walk through the streets, perusing every single stall and wishing I had five bags full of gold coins to spend in this place. Both the Imen and the Maras had developed a fascinating culture here, complete with a plethora of significant objects and customs. From what I could see, the Imen were more focused on the gastronomic side of things, along with the raw materials for different handcrafting and art projects, while the Maras devoted most of their resources to the end results, offering visitors an impressive range of decorative objects. It was a much-needed distraction that didn't really alter Azure Heights' regular functions, but rather enriched them, as people could skip work for an hour or so, just to browse through the stalls.

Patrik and I wandered through the fair for a couple of hours, looking around while searching for the ingredients he needed for his ambitious spell aimed at the asteroid belt.

I occasionally stole glances at him as he exchanged words with different herb and crystal sellers. The memory of our kiss from the day before refused to go away.

"So, when are we going to try this spell, provided you find everything you need here?" I asked, as Patrik thanked an Iman merchant and we resumed our slow walk through the fair.

"It will definitely have to wait until evening," Patrik replied. "We need a clear night sky for this to work. The asteroid belt needs to be visible."

I couldn't help but gaze at the crowd around us, watching as both Imen and Maras went about their business, buying and selling to one another, offering brief smiles and compliments over the quality of the merchandise on sale. There was a noticeable difference between the two species where demeanor was concerned.

The Imen were soft and humble, as opposed to the sharp and confident attitude of the Maras. The contrast was interesting to watch in a large crowd, as I could observe different groups displaying similar patterns of behavior. The Maras clearly considered themselves superior—one could tell from the way they looked at the Imen, the short periods of eye contact they made with them, and the comparatively few words they used when addressing them.

"I mean, it's still a long shot, but it's worth a try," Patrik continued.

We walked around for a little while longer, wondering how much of the Imen's softness was genuinely theirs, and how much of it had been implanted via mind-bending. It was reasonable for me to question the reality at this point, knowing what we knew about the complicated relationship between the two species. After all, we knew for a fact that the Maras had been using their mind-bending for more than just psychotherapeutic purposes.

The silence between Patrik and me started to feel awkward. I had nothing and everything to tell him. And yet, as much as I wanted to address what I had done yesterday, I couldn't find the right words to form a single coherent sentence.

He seemed to sense my internal anguish somehow. He looked at me and exhaled, putting his hands in his pockets. "Scarlett, I... I'm sorry I haven't brought this up. We should've talked about this already, but... I haven't been able to find the right words."

The more he stuttered, fumbling through the phrases as he tried to talk about our kiss, the more I realized that Patrik was having a hard time expressing himself on the matter. If anything, he was just as nervous as I was about it, maybe even more so. It was downright adorable, watching him—the tall, devastatingly handsome, and intelligent Druid—trying... well, endearingly failing to talk to a girl. Specifically, a girl he'd already acknowledged that he could see. And we both knew what he'd meant by that.

"I mean, I just wanted you to know... Scarlett, what you did —what *we* did yesterday... I didn't expect it to..." Patrik tried again, just as clumsy an attempt as the first one.

I, on the other hand, was feeling braver than ever before. The energy I'd felt flowing through me the day before, back at the library, had come back, stronger and brighter. It was enough to jolt me into doing the unspeakable again.

"In fact, I just wanted to... I don't know why it's so difficult to—" he muttered, and I moved to face him, stopping him in his tracks. I cupped his face with my hands and pulled him into another kiss.

The moment our lips touched, I closed my eyes and welcomed the incandescent sparkles invading my consciousness. I held my breath, as he opened his mouth and became an active participant, taking over and completely dazzling me.

He responded, deepening the kiss and wrapping his arms

around me. He pulled me closer, and I had no other choice but to rest my hands on his shoulders and welcome the amazing taste of him. His tongue skillfully worked mine, and my blood simmered, my pulse starting to race through my veins.

This changed everything. I wasn't really sure what I had intended by kissing him again, but it had resulted in something truly extraordinary. I melted in his arms, feeling echoes of his thudding heart inside my chest as he kissed me with everything he had. It was as if he'd been waiting forever to do this, much like me, for that matter.

From the moment I had first laid eyes on Patrik, I'd felt my heart flutter and my stomach tighten, and the more time we'd spent together, the more intense my feelings toward him became. I couldn't help but shudder in his embrace, so happy that this was happening, and yet still wrapping my head around it. He felt that, and tightened his grip, bringing one hand up to hold the back of my head as he pulled me even closer, and even deeper into our kiss.

It didn't matter that we were surrounded by strange creatures, some of whom could be hostile, as far as we knew. It didn't matter that we were stuck on this planet with no means of reaching out to GASP or our families. It didn't even matter that there were daemons out there, eager to eat our souls and destroy the city.

In the midst of it all, Patrik and I had somehow found each other. And for the first time in months, he seemed to have put the thought of Kyana aside and followed his instincts. More importantly, for the first time in my life, I was kissing the creature I had hopelessly and irrevocably fallen in love with.

I knew that we were going to have to talk about it, at some point. But, for the time being, all I could do was welcome him into my life, and into my heart, as we kissed in the middle of a narrow alley at the Spring Fair.

## 13

## AVRIL

### (DAUGHTER OF LUCAS & MARION)

After we were done with our in-depth study of Lemuel's archives, we stashed the scrolls and ancient registries away, pulling the bookshelf back to cover the opening in the wall. We then snuck out, making sure to lock the door to the old Iman's studio after us.

"We still have some time to kill before evening falls," Heron said, then nodded toward the alley that led deeper into the first level of the city. "We might as well go on a stroll and check things out."

"Yeah, I'm just bummed out that Lemuel's hidden archival treasure didn't tell us more about the Maras and the asteroid belt," I replied as we walked.

"I don't know why I'm saying this, but I have a feeling it

would've been too easy if we'd found all the answers tucked away inside some slum wall here," Heron muttered.

"What do you mean by 'too easy'?"

"It's just that... It doesn't look like this city will give away all of its secrets at once. Something inside me says we won't get to the bottom of this as quickly as we'd hoped."

"Do you think the Maras have something to do with it? With this feeling of yours, I mean?" I asked, looking around at the buzzing crowd of Imen moving up and down the road. The wary looks that they gave us made me think that we were definitely onto something, as far as the Maras' behavior and mind-bending practice were concerned.

"Could be," Heron replied, "but it would be just conjecture at this point, without any proof. And I'm not one to buy into shabby conspiracy theories. I mean, sure, I definitely don't trust the Maras, and we both know there is something fishy going on here, but unless we can back our suspicions up with real facts, we're just speculating."

"I agree, but I've also been taught to listen to my instincts when pursuing a line of inquiry, and I think you should do the same. If your gut is telling you something, then please do share, so we can put our heads together and uncover whatever form of foul play the Maras are up to."

Heron gave me an appreciative half-smile as we reached the end of the alley and turned left. Clay brick houses lined both sides of the road ahead, with small windows and charcoal slate roofs. This wasn't the snazzier side of town, but it wasn't a slum either. My guess was that the majority of Imen living here were of lower to middle class, most likely working service jobs higher up in the city. "We might as well check out the Spring Fair, since we're out," Heron suggested, and I replied with a brief nod.

There were more Correction Officers out and about, patrolling the streets in pairs. Since Patrick's protection spell had failed to keep the daemons out, the guards were on high alert. I could tell, from the looks on their faces, that there was tension between them.

"Don't they look gloomier than usual?" I muttered to Heron. He narrowed his eyes, paying attention to a specific pair that passed by. The sideways glances that they gave us sent chills down my spine. They made me feel as though we weren't exactly welcome here, as if *we* were the intruders, and not the daemons that we were trying to protect everyone from.

"They must be on edge. Although we both know that some of these scowls have nothing to do with the failed protection spell," Heron replied, his voice low. "They're definitely keeping secrets from us, but unfortunately we cannot accuse them directly of withholding information, especially where the treatment of Imen is concerned."

"Yeah, I know. Still... I would love to shake them up a little bit and get to the bottom of this," I murmured, pressing my arms over my chest.

"Trust me, I'm right there with you on that one, but it will get the Imen in trouble if we go about it *our* way."

We briefly looked at each other, exchanging knowing smirks as we made a left turn, then took the stairs up to the fourth level. The Spring Fair was a huge, open market, spreading over the entire neighborhood. The awnings were pulled all the way over the small square in front of us, and stalls lined all four sides. There was plenty of food on display, along with artisanal confectionery, baked goods, handmade sweets, oils, and syrups.

"This must be one of the food markets that we've heard about, part of the fair," I said as we toured the place. The market was full of Imen, mostly females with their children, while the males were holed up in taverns nearby—I could hear them laughing and clinking glasses. It turned out they weren't that different from the humans back on Earth.

"Wow, this is one of the few times when I actually wish I could eat something," Heron muttered, his jade eyes wandering around the multitude of pastries, buttered breads, and jams on display.

"At least they have a rich culture in terms of gastronomy," I replied. "I wonder how much of their true heritage has been deleted through mind-bending."

"We have to be extremely diplomatic and discreet if we want to learn anything from these people. I don't doubt that there are Maras eavesdropping, wherever we go," Heron whispered in my ear. "Chances are that they're listening as we speak."

"So, what, I should let them intimidate us into not asking the right questions?" I raised an eyebrow at him.

"Nope, not at all." He smirked. "If anything, I say we make ourselves heard, loud and clear, so they know that we are not to be played with. Although, I was hoping we'd already proven that by coming back from those gorges alive and in one piece —twice."

I caught glimpses of dark shadows rushing through adjacent streets, but nothing too precise. Nevertheless, I knew that there were Correction Officers patrolling the area, and, as Heron had suggested, they were most likely following us.

"Maybe they're not that easy to impress," I quipped, and he chuckled. We reached the other side of the food market. The crowd buzzed, the Imen walking around filling their baskets with food and syrup bottles in exchange for handfuls of silver and copper pennies.

We didn't even see Cadmus until I nearly walked into him. We both stopped, just inches away from him. I hadn't expected to see him here, in these parts of the city, as he was one of Caspian's most trusted lieutenants, and mostly assigned to the upper parts—specifically the top levels, where the Lords resided and did their business.

His expression was firm, and dark lines gathered between his brows as he frowned at us.

"Cadmus, I didn't expect to see you here," I said politely.

He gave us both a brief nod, keeping his hands behind his back and his chin up.

"I, on the other hand, knew exactly where to find you," he replied bluntly.

"That really doesn't come as a surprise." Heron scoffed, glancing around. "This place is riddled with your people."

"Lord Kifo did leave me in command, but rest assured that I cannot keep track of all of my officers. The Lords and other superiors from the five families also have authority over the guards."

"What is it that you're trying to say?" I asked, and he gave me a stern look.

"Watch your backs. You have aroused the interest of many, in a city that is still recovering from the explosions. There are eyes on you at all times. And none of them answer to me," Cadmus said.

"I'm not following you." I shook my head, not clear on what his message was.

"The city is not what it seems," Cadmus replied, "and poking around things that have long been buried won't do you any good."

I realized what he was referring to. Someone knew where we'd been. Even worse, someone knew what we had been looking at. Was it just me, or were Lemuel's archives not that big of a secret? Did Cadmus know? I couldn't ask him directly —I would risk exposing the studio and its contents, if he didn't know and was just fishing.

"You know, being so cryptic won't do you any good," Heron muttered, his gaze fixed on Cadmus. "I'll have you know we don't really care who's looking, or who's listening. We are here to do our jobs, and that involves asking uncomfortable questions, poking at people who would very much prefer not to be poked, and digging through the dirt until all your secrets come out and we discover everything about your city, your servants, and your practices—unethical or otherwise. Am I making myself clear?"

"Is that your way of telling me that you will not be intimidated?" Cadmus replied, the corner of his mouth twitching.

Heron took a step forward, bringing himself close enough to invade Cadmus's personal space, asserting himself as the challenging force. "You're damn right we're not going to be intimidated. If anything, the harder you come after us, the more it will hurt you when we strike back."

They stood like that for about a minute, death stares and all, until Cadmus broke eye contact and gave me a brief smile.

"That's good to hear," he breathed, then walked away.

It took us a few moments to understand what had just happened. We both turned around and watched Cadmus disappear into the crowd of Imen. I then looked at Heron, raising an eyebrow.

"What was all that about?" I asked.

"I honestly have no idea, but the dude switched from hot to cold way too fast." Heron shrugged.

"So, he was what... testing us? Trying to see if he could intimidate us? To what end?"

"Maybe he has something to tell us, but doesn't know if we

are ready to hear it. Or, worse, maybe he doesn't know if he can trust us. I certainly wouldn't trust someone who is easily frightened or derailed," Heron said.

"Yeah, well, whatever it is, I'm damn tired of all these cryptic replies, of all their secrets and weird habits. Tired, in fact, doesn't even begin to cover it," I replied, my teeth gritting as I resumed our walk through the market.

Whatever came next, it most likely involved the Maras. With every day that passed, it felt as though we were getting both closer and farther away from the truth. It was bad enough that I was worried about Harper and her team, out there, infiltrating the daemon city... I certainly didn't have any more patience for half-truths and Mara secrets that could very well get us in more trouble.

Cadmus was hiding something. Not that it was a surprise, but he had just made sure that we knew it. Sooner or later, we were going to meet again and expand on what had just happened. Specifically, on what he had just told us—in not very many words.

What did transpire from our brief exchange was that we now knew there were eyes on us at all times, that we had stirred the pot, and that, as we'd suspected, this city held plenty of secrets. And I was determined to uncover each and every one of them, until they led me to a way off this damn planet.

Whether it was the Maras, or the daemons, or whoever else who thought we should stay here indefinitely, it didn't matter. All that mattered to me was that we get to the bottom of it, then hop in a light bubble and fly back home.

# 14

## FIONA

### (DAUGHTER OF BENEDICT & YELENA)

After a brief visit to the library, to check through the service records of the Lords' mansions, I learned that Arrah's father hailed from one of the neighborhoods on the third level. The servants' places of birth were the few snippets of Imen information that I could find in that library.

I figured it was as good a place as any to look around, and see if I could find anything, or meet anyone who might know something about Arrah and her whereabouts. I spent a couple of hours walking through the narrow alleys, keeping my ears open. Sooner or later, someone could say something of interest to someone else—something of interest to me, at least.

Despite the Spring Fair, there were plenty of Imen out and about, most of them working in different stores and bars in the area. I tried to be as inconspicuous as possible, keeping to the side streets and the shadows as I listened in on various conversations. There were plenty of rumors flying around—about us, about the daemons, and, most importantly, about the aftermath of the attacks on the Lords' mansions.

The Imen were mourning the loss of their friends and extended family members who had lost their lives in the explosions. Some of them, specifically a group of young females, brought up Arrah's name, along with her brother's.

"She was always a strange girl," one of the females said, shaking her head slowly, "but she certainly didn't deserve such grief. It was bad enough that she never knew her father. To then lose her mother to daemons, her brother to prison... and now her whole life, her little home inside the Roho mansion, destroyed."

"It just doesn't seem fair," another replied. "My mother went up to the South Bend Inn this morning to talk to her, to see how she was doing. You see, our mothers were good friends. But Arrah was nowhere to be found. Nobody knows where she went."

"Speaking of which," a third Iman girl interjected, "did you hear that her brother escaped from jail?"

I froze. Sure, the Correction Officers had been bound to discover that Demios was gone, but it still made me feel nervous. No one could have even guessed that I'd been the one to let him out. But when you have a conscience, no matter the endgame, you still feel a little guilty for breaking the rules.

The first one gasped. "How do you know?"

"My friend, Maia, is a servant in the Kifo mansion," the third replied. "She specifically services Lord Kifo and his lieutenants, the ones in charge of the prison. She overheard them when one of the Correction Officers reported Demios missing this morning."

"Oh my, do they think that has something to do with Arrah's disappearance?" the second Iman girl asked. "What if they both ran away together? What if Demios got out, found his sister at the South Bend Inn, then left the city with her?"

"I hope they didn't. It's such a dangerous world out there." The first girl sighed. "Now that we know the daemons are real... I would hate for something to happen to Arrah and her brother."

"I don't know," the second one muttered. "Maybe they're better off out there, beyond the gorges, in the western plains with the Free People."

"Don't say that!"

"Why not?" The second girl defended herself. "We're all thinking it. Ever since our people started disappearing, we've all been thinking it. Maybe it *is* time for us to consider leaving. The tribes in the western plains would surely welcome us with arms wide open."

"Shut up, Alla! Our lords don't look kindly upon sedition!" the first Iman girl hissed. "You'll get yourself *and us* in trouble with such thoughts!"

Several seconds went by, and I inched forward from my little hiding spot around the corner, just so I could get a better look at the three girls. They were dressed in simple, modest black dresses, their hair caught up in conservative buns. They were seated around a table outside a café, sipping tea. The fearful looks in their eyes told me everything I needed to know. The Maras clearly didn't like it when their servants thought of leaving the city—and that was in direct contradiction to what Emilian had told us before.

"Get those ideas out of your head," the first Iman girl said, her voice low as she scowled at her friend, who stared at the cobblestone beneath her feet.

"You don't want to be heard by the wrong people. You know what happens when the wrong people hear you," the third one added.

My stomach churned, as I realized then that the Maras were definitely hiding something with regards to their treatment of the Imen. We had been speculating before. We'd noticed the discrepancies and blanked-out memories. But this was the first time that I was hearing an Iman specifically warn another Iman about the Maras. Who else could they mean by "wrong people", anyway?

While I had no new lead on Arrah, at least I had managed to confirm what we'd already suspected. This wasn't exactly the artful and joyful democracy that we'd been told it was. It was starting to sound more and more like an authoritarian regime. My only question at this point was how severe it actually was.

What price did an Iman pay for leaving the city? What

punishment was there for what the girls had referred to as sedition?

A thud startled me, and tore gasps from the Imen girls. I followed their gazes to a male Iman, who had collapsed in the middle of the square. Others gathered quickly around him, some crouching to touch his face and get a feel for his temperature, while murmurs arose from the growing crowd.

The Imen girls stayed put, their hands gripping the armrests of their chairs. They watched the entire scene unfold with deep frowns. My first instinct was to go out and check on the Iman lying on the ground, but a couple of Correction Officers beat me to it. I didn't move, my eyes fixed on the two Maras.

They pushed the people away, then picked the collapsed Iman up and carried him down the stairs leading to the second level—they were taking him to the infirmary. The others watched, a mixture of fear and curiosity imprinted on their pale faces. None had the courage to object, and yet all of them showed genuine concern.

"He's, what, the fifth one this week?" the first Iman girl from the café murmured.

"I don't know... I've lost track," the third one breathed.

"It's been happening more frequently over the past few years," the second Iman girl, the slightly more rebellious one, said, leaning against the back of her chair with a sullen expression.

"What could it be that's making the slumber before death

claim so many of our people in such high numbers these days?" the first one replied.

"We will never find out, and you both know it. I think the better question to ask is: what would it take for us to get out of here?" the *rebel* said. Once again, her friends glowered at her, warning her to keep quiet and not get herself in any trouble.

There were few people around them, but I saw at least one giving them a suspicious sideways glance as he passed by. As much as I would've loved to just go out there and talk to them, it was too risky—not so much for me, but for them.

The girls were right. The city had ears.

## 15

## HANSA

**W**e were about a hundred yards away from the meranium box in the east wing, based on Harper's assessments and the distance we'd covered so far, carefully sneaking behind statues and curtains as we avoided daemon guards moving down the corridor. Jax had managed to snatch a couple more of those red lenses on the way—much more discreetly than I had managed in my previous endeavor.

We stilled as two more daemons passed us, muttering to each other about the difficulties of their jobs.

"I swear, it has all gone crazy since those outsiders came here," one of them said, then cursed under his breath.

"The king wants them alive," the second one replied. "It takes a bit more work, but we have to do it. Put the lens on. You heard what the counselor said. They could be here."

The daemon did as he was told, mounting the red lens between his cheek and eyebrow, like an old-fashioned monocle. The elder Druids back on Calliope used to wear the same, albeit in clear glass, to help them see better as their eyes began to suffer the downsides of age. He glanced around, and I pulled myself back behind the statue to stay out of sight.

"I don't get it," the red lens daemon sighed. "Why does he need them alive? Why can't we just kill them? Or better yet, why can't we just eat their souls?"

"Don't be stupid! The king wants them alive; therefore we will capture them, *alive*. And even if we were allowed to eat their souls, you're a lowly guard. The king and the princes get first dibs."

"You know," the red lens daemon replied, slightly amused, "my father said things were different back in the old days, when Shaytan's father held the throne. He said we had it much better as... lowly guards."

The other daemon smacked the back of his head, hard enough to make him yelp.

"If you want to get yourself killed, keep talking like that, you idiot. But don't drag me down with you by telling me such nonsense. We serve *this* king, not his father. Know your allegiance!"

"Oh, come on," the red lens daemon shot back. "We both know that the kingdom is much shoddier now than it was five thousand years ago! The pacifists are stronger, and we both know that there is an uprising coming his way!"

"Okay, smartass, then who will you bet on? The almighty king, with his army of daemons, generals, death claws, pit wolves, and magic? Or a handful of weaklings, who have simply gotten better at passing messages to one another throughout the city?"

"They are smarter than you think."

"I keep telling you to stop being so gullible and downright stupid, and yet you go and double down on this nonsense," the backhanding daemon shot back. They moved forward, and farther away from us. "The king will crush them eventually. We already have Mose. After him, the others will fall like saplings in a thunderstorm."

They continued arguing as they patrolled the hallway, but the main takeaway from their conversation was quite clear: the daemons had minds of their own. Not all of them agreed with Shaytan. However, his armed forces had bigger numbers, and had a pretty good chance of crushing any rebellion. At the same time, with a little help from us, perhaps the "pacifists" could, eventually, overthrow this evil regime, and maybe even rescue their fallen brothers, Mose included, from jail.

"Let's keep moving," Jax whispered, then found my hand and pulled me after him as he shortened the distance to the meranium box.

The sound of footsteps behind us prompted us to swiftly hide behind another statue, crouching so that its base could keep us covered from any red lenses. I couldn't see much from that angle, but the three pairs of feet that passed by were not those of guards. I caught glimpses of smooth leather and gold buckles, snugly tied around thick, muscular calves.

They went inside the hall next to us, and their voices echoed into the hallway.

"Ah, it took you a while to get here," Shaytan's voice boomed, sending chills down my spine. I immediately stood and tiptoed to the doorframe, peeking into the large, sumptuously gilded hall. We had actually reached the throne room— and it was truly a gorgeous sight to behold, with lavish velvet drapes covering the massive, floor-to-ceiling windows, gold and gemstone embellishments covering the walls, and, of course, the enormous throne, sculpted entirely out of black obsidian, and tastefully adorned with more gold and perfect diamonds.

Several servants stood quietly, lining the walls on both sides of the throne, while his two counselors—judging by their elegant, yet non-regal attire—settled by one of the windows. Shaytan sank into his throne, letting out a long sigh of relief, and leaned into the soft pillows behind him.

My heart stopped beating as soon as I laid eyes on the figure standing in the middle of the hall. My hand instinctively caught Jax's wrist, squeezing tightly. I tried to keep my mouth shut, but my blood instantly boiled.

"Yes, well, the gorges are never kind to a Mara," Darius replied with a smirk.

He was alive. Dressed in his usual luxurious silk garments, Darius didn't look as though he'd been charred in a fire. If anything, he was glowing, his lips stretching into a satisfied grin. I swallowed a curse, trying to figure out what was going on. The Lord of House Xunn had been identified among the remains that we had retrieved from the devastated mansions. We'd seen his Lordship ring. We'd literally held his funeral service earlier that morning!

And yet, there he was, breathing and kicking, and a guest in daemon city.

"Don't be so dramatic," Shaytan replied, his fingers tapping the armrest. "All my subjects know not to touch you."

"Not all of them. But don't worry, I made sure they were brought up to speed," Darius retorted.

"I hope you left them alive."

That hadn't been a casual remark. A threat bubbled beneath it—I could tell from the lower tone that the king of daemons had used.

"They're alive, Your Grace." Darius bowed reverently, and Shaytan responded with a nod. "Thank you for having me over."

"It's not like you had anywhere else to go." The king smirked.

"Yes, well, desperate times." Darius shook his head. "And speaking of desperate measures, where is the rest of the GASP team that came over? Have they been captured?"

I felt Jax's arm snake around my waist. He was ready to hold me back, because he knew exactly what my first instinct was—to immediately go out there and cut Darius's head off. It took a couple of seconds of deep breaths and additional focus to keep myself under control, and to stifle the rage that was pouring through me.

Darius had faked his death. Did his daughter know? She couldn't... She'd been devastated. I'd seen it in her eyes, on her face. I didn't know how she could have faked that kind of raw pain. Her grief was all too familiar. Whatever this was, I wasn't sure it involved the others.

Had he gone rogue? Had he been talking to Shaytan? Were they in cahoots, somehow?

"Let us call it a work in progress," the king replied.

The Mara had something to do with this. We were being hunted, and he was one of the masterminds behind it all. I had trouble wrapping my head around this. It was a development I simply hadn't seen coming. Who could've? I mean, I'd watched his funeral pyre burn until there was nothing left but ashes, his daughter standing by the side, holding his Lordship ring and crying her heart out.

"How long until you catch them?" Darius asked. A slight frown pulled his brows together as he briefly glanced at the two counselors by the window. Neither of them looked pleased to see him there, but it didn't look as if they had any other choice but to tolerate his presence.

"Obviously, the sooner the better, but I cannot possibly predict anything at this point. My soldiers will get them. I have something they want." Shaytan grinned. "And from what you've told me, they don't leave any of their own behind."

*Son of a...*

"Good. I don't feel comfortable kicking off the next stage of our plan with those four running around, all loose and what-not. I cannot guarantee the safety of my people while the succubus and her acolytes roam free," Darius replied.

I gripped the handle of my broadsword, squeezing tightly as another means of preventing myself from attacking him right here and now.

"Do not worry, my friend. At least we have the dragon and the fae," the king said. "It renders the others less effective, without their firepower. They are virtually useless without the dragon."

"We can both agree on that. They haven't left the city, though, have they?" Darius asked.

"Like I said, they will try to come for their people. They are not leaving the city. Not of their own accord, or mine. All the tunnel exits are guarded."

"I trust your judgment, Your Grace." The Mara bowed curtly, keeping his hands behind his back. "Now, if you'll excuse me, I'm a little peckish. Let us meet again in the morning and catch up. Perhaps, by then, you'll have the others in a meranium box."

"Of course, make yourself at home," the king replied. "I shall see you again in the morning."

Jax pulled me back behind the statue as Darius came out of the throne room and walked down the hallway, toward the north side of the palace. I breathed out, still stunned from everything we had just witnessed.

"Should we go after him?" I whispered to Jax. "Whatever he's planning, we need to know. We need to find out. It's not just our lives at stake here. The others are back in Azure Heights, and they have no idea."

"We're better off focusing on Blaze and Caia at this point, Hansa," he breathed. "No doubt, whatever Darius is doing, we'll need to warn the others. And that includes the Maras who are out there mourning his death."

There was no time for us to further discuss this. Jax was right. Blaze and Caia were our priority, and they weren't too far away, either—provided we were on the right side of the palace. We had to get them out first, escape this wretched city, make it out to the western plains, and regroup there.

This wasn't my first taste of betrayal, either. Although, the last time I had been double-crossed, I had lost many of my sisters and daughters. I had buried that grief, and focused on revenge. There was a lot of darkness and anger boiling inside me, and Darius's actions had brought it all back to the surface.

My muscles ached, as did my heart, and fear gripped my throat with its cold, icy claws. I couldn't bear to lose anyone again. Not Jax, not Blaze or Caia, not Harper or Fiona, or anyone else for that matter. I was done burying my loved ones because some asshole chose to betray me and his own people.

Just as I had cut off Goren's head during our war against

Azazel, I knew my broadsword would soon taste the blood of Darius Xunn.

# 16

# HARPER

## (DAUGHTER OF HAZEL & TEJUS)

As Zane went about his business throughout the western wing of the palace, Caspian and I stayed close, but always out of sight. The daemons in possession of red garnet were wearing the lenses at all times, making it a little bit more difficult for us to sneak around. Fortunately, Shaytan's palace furnishings were numerous and large enough to conceal us.

Zane exchanged a few words with various guards, which helped us find out more about their positions, their orders, and their overall state. Most of them weren't all too happy with having to look for us, and some of them seemed to be quite fond of Zane, as the youngest and friendliest of the princes. He seemed to have a good relationship with the soldiers. Based on

their remarks alone, Zane's brothers were the textbook definition of entitled jerks.

"Just keep your eyes open," Zane told two of the guards as
they moved farther down the hallway and away from us. "If I
were you, I'd focus more on the northern wing, particularly on
the ground floor, since the outsiders will most likely come
through there."

The daemons nodded and continued their patrol, while
Zane went deeper into the first floor of the western wing. We
followed him, quietly, as he took us into a massive hall, and I
found myself holding my breath for a couple of seconds,
marveling at the stunning beauty around me. The place was
huge, and hot baths and water canals were carved into the
black stone floor, right in the middle.

Large steps allowed smooth access to our level, and wildflowers, layers of colorful silk, and soft satin cushions were
scattered all over. Amber lights glimmered from the overhead
chandeliers, giant contraptions made of pure gold and loaded
with perfectly polished crystals. Dozens of daemon females
sauntered around, their bodies scantily covered in red and
gold silk, with gemstones adorning their long and curved
horns. The majority were relatively young, but there were
slightly more mature females resting around a firepit.

The one thing they all had in common was the joy they
seemed to experience at the sight of Zane, who put on a broad
smile and offered them a courteous and ample bow. They all
hummed and giggled, some of them gathering around him

and dropping kisses on both his cheeks. Zane seemed to be the apple of their eyes, but he was the center of the universe to one specific daemon female. She stood up from her clique by the firepit and put her arms out with a radiant smile.

In some ways, she reminded me of Grandma Sofia, her timeless beauty and grace amplified by her luxurious garments, not to mention her long, ink-black hair, flowing freely down her back. Her bright red eyes lit up as Zane walked over and wrapped his arms around her, holding her tight. I realized then that her incandescent expression was one of pride. I had already figured out that Zane was surprisingly influential and loved in this place—but the adoration pouring out of this daemon female, in particular, was genuinely heart-warming.

It showed the daemons in a different light. For a split second, it didn't feel as though we were surrounded by blood-thirsty fiends eager to eat our souls. They seemed capable of intense and positive emotions. It made me wonder how many of them were truly murderous, and how many were simply forced to obey their king.

"My darling," the female daemon purred, caressing his face. "It is so nice of you to come see me."

"It's always a pleasure, Mother," Zane replied gently, then briefly glanced our way, as if quietly introducing us to his mother. "How is life in the harem these days?"

"It's the same thing every day, my darling." She sighed. "I'm one of the fortunate ones, as your father no longer has any business with me. Me and my elderly sisters, we hang out by the fire, bathe in the hot waters, and teach the younglings how to best please the king."

"I take it he's taken a new wife?" Zane muttered, glancing toward a group of young females at the far left corner of the hall. The one in the middle was wide-eyed and seemed out of place, her gaze darting around, glimmers of fear making it clear that she'd yet to get accustomed to her new "home".

"He hasn't told you, has he?" There was a tinge of sadness in his mother's voice. "It's okay, Zane. We will take good care of her."

"Just make sure she doesn't become another Luella," Zane breathed, shaking his head slowly. "I don't know what I will do if she ends up the same way."

"It's been two years, my darling. You have to stop blaming yourself for what happened. Luella had a strong spirit, and your father was well aware of that when he brought her over. It's on him, and only him. Some creatures are simply too wild to be tamed."

Zane measured the new female from head to toe for about a minute, before shifting his focus back to his mother.

"She's... what, his fourth this year?" he asked.

"You know how he gets when he's anxious," his mother replied. "A wife always soothes him; hence a harem that keeps growing makes your father happy."

"How long has she been here?"

I took a better look at the young female daemon in question. Her hair was long and fiery red, braided with strips of black leather, and she'd been squeezed into a tight, tan leather dress, its shade lighter than her skin. Her lips were full and soft, her red eyes inquisitive, and her hands balled into fists at her sides. The mixture of fear and anger drawing shadows on her round face was all too familiar. She was the ferocious tigress captured by poachers and stuffed into a cage—albeit an enclosure covered in gold and gemstones.

Shaytan had plenty of wives, and continued to get more... It said a lot of things about him, and none were positive. He was definitely a big, strong, highly feared and respected ruler, and yet he needed the feminine softness in his life—as much of it as possible. I figured it could, at some point, be used against him.

"Just a couple of days, my darling," his mother replied. "Of course, she isn't happy to be here, but we are doing our best to keep her safe. All she needs to do is listen to us, and she will survive."

"I'm surprised he hasn't told me about her. I don't think he told anyone... He usually revels in his wedding ceremonies and lavish dinners," Zane scoffed.

"With everything that has been going on, and especially after what happened to Luella, I'm not surprised at all that he didn't tell you." She gave him a weak smile. "He is afraid of you, you know."

"What are you talking about, Mother? He just threatened to exile and kill me if I don't get in line and play along."

"Exactly, my darling. He wouldn't care about what you have to say if he were not afraid of you. He saw how Luella changed you... He will never admit it, though. Your father is a proud daemon, but believe me when I tell you he fears you more than any of his sons. Don't let him think he has any power over you."

Zane took a step forward, inching closer to his mother so he could whisper in her ear. "Be careful what you say, Mother. These walls have ears, and you know how much the king loves to eavesdrop on his ladies."

She hugged him again, then nodded at Shaytan's newest wife, gesturing for her to come closer. The young female frowned, but listened, and walked over to Zane's mother's side. She put an arm around the younger daemon's shoulders.

"Now, if you'll excuse me, Ondine's new quarters are ready." She winked at her son. "I'll leave you to your business, my darling. Just be careful."

"You too," Zane replied. "Don't get yourselves into any trouble. The king's fuse is short these days."

He bid them farewell, then walked back out to the hallway. Caspian and I followed, keeping to the side, so we could jump behind any of the statues and pillars ahead if more daemons passed by.

"How many wives does your father have?" I asked.

"I don't know." Zane shrugged. "I lost track."

"What do they do all day? Does he visit them every day?

Do they take turns? How does this work? Do you know how many sons he has, how many brothers you have?"

"Is she always this curious, Lord Kifo?" Zane muttered.

"What, you two know each other?" I shot back. Caspian and I used the red lenses we'd snagged earlier from the guards to look at each other. He gave me a brief scowl, before looking ahead.

"I didn't say that," Zane replied. "I just make a habit of knowing everyone who sets foot into my kingdom."

"*Your* kingdom?"

"I am a prince, after all. I may not be entitled to the crown, once the king passes away, but this is still my land; these are still my people. This is, for all intents and purposes, my kingdom."

I tried to use my reading skills on him. Even as a sentry, I didn't seem to have access to his emotions—that had already been made clear, repeatedly, from our previous encounters with daemons. Nevertheless, I focused a little harder, just to see if I could get a feel for what he was experiencing in that moment. Unfortunately, I didn't get anything from him. Either he was very well guarded by nature, emotionally speaking, or there was no way at all for a sentry to tap into a daemon's heart.

However, it didn't take a scientist or a super sentry to figure out the basics: Zane, though a prince, didn't have a good relationship with his father; his mother, on the other hand, meant the world to him. In fact, Zane was much more appreciated around the castle than any of his brothers. The females—the king's wives, to be precise—adored him. On top of that, he was helping us get our friends back.

I had a feeling that we had a much stronger ally in Zane than I'd originally thought. And after all the losses and painful twists and turns, we really needed a win.

# 17

# HARPER

## (DAUGHTER OF HAZEL & TEJUS)

About half an hour later, Zane brought us to the meranium box. It looked weird from the outside, lodged inside the obsidian wall in an adjacent chamber. We were hidden behind a large pit wolf statue, waiting for the guards to change.

I leaned forward, just enough to get a better look inside the chamber. It was an empty space, except for the meranium box and the four soldiers armed with rapiers and red lenses, which they hadn't put on yet. Zane walked in just as four more daemons left, splitting into pairs and going in opposite directions down the hallway.

My True Sight didn't work on the meranium box, not even from thirty feet away. But deep down I knew that Caia and Blaze were in there. My instinct was screaming at me.

"How's it going?" Zane asked in a casual tone, walking over to one of the guards, and setting our attack plan in motion.

"My lord." The daemon nodded respectfully. "All good. No signs of the outsiders."

"Yeah, I'm not surprised," he replied. "I get the feeling that you won't see any... signs."

"We are ready for them," another guard said, keeping his chin up in defiance. "Besides, all the guards outside are actively patrolling. We will get them, sooner or later."

"What can I say?" Zane shrugged nonchalantly, feigning disinterest as he threw me a glance over his shoulder. "I appreciate your confidence, but, like I said, I doubt that you will see them coming..."

He chuckled. That was the signal phrase that Caspian and I had been waiting for. We'd already agreed on it, fifteen minutes earlier, with Zane. We both hurried out, quietly taking up positions in front of the first two guards, while Zane was already facing the third, with the fourth to his right.

I didn't look straight at mine, to avoid him catching a glimpse of my eyes, given the faulty invisibility spell. We'd moved so fast that they hadn't even noticed the air rippling around us.

But all four of them looked somewhat confused, frowning at Zane.

"What do you mean, my lord?" the daemon in front of me asked.

"I'm just saying, you guys need to pay more attention. I

thought the king ordered you all to wear your red lenses at all times." Zane shook his head in disappointment.

The daemon to his right cursed under his breath and fumbled with his lens, mounting it over his eye. He stilled, staring right at us, as the others prepared to put theirs on, as well. With lightning speed, I drove my twin swords through my daemon's throat, while Caspian beheaded his with one swift move.

The one facing Zane didn't stand a chance, either. He dropped to his knees, gurgling blood, as Zane pulled his long knife from his chest. Before the fourth guard could make a move, I dashed over and brought my swords down.

He was fast enough to block one of them with his cuffed forearm, but he couldn't stop the other from digging into his left shoulder. He growled from the pain, but I didn't give him the chance to counterattack. In the rage of the moment, I sank my fangs into his throat and tore it out, and he fell backward.

Arterial spray shot out, and he desperately tried to stop the enormous amount of blood gushing out of him, but ten seconds later, he gave his last breath. I licked my lips and tasted daemon blood.

"Well, that was harsh!" Zane exclaimed, staring at me in disbelief.

"It seemed easier from that angle." I shrugged, then wiped the rest of the blood from my chin with my sleeve. I couldn't afford to be spotted because of a blood smear. "Can you see it? Is there any left on me?"

Zane squinted, one eye narrowed through a red lens, then shook his head. "I have to say, I like your style."

"You and me both," Caspian replied, blinking rapidly, his eyebrows arched with surprise. "Didn't know you had it in you."

"You ain't seen nothin' yet." I gave them both a faint smirk, then shifted my focus to the meranium box in front of us.

Its surface was perfectly polished, a smooth and reflective gloss that showed only one figure—Zane, as Caspian and I were still very much invisible. And beyond that layer of metal, impervious to my True Sight, were my friends.

At the center of the cube facing us, at approximately my height, was a square hatch. It looked barely big enough for me to go through. I reached out to touch it, but Zane slapped my hand away.

"There's swamp witch magic at work here," he said, and my scowl faded quickly. "You're of no use right now. Let me take care of this, then you can hug and kiss your friends, or whatever."

"What are you doing?" I asked.

"Deactivating the magic keeping your friends' fires at bay."

He leaned forward toward the metal surface and whispered something under his breath. Hundreds of swamp witch symbols lit up, incandescent charms embedded into the meranium. Zane was right—I wouldn't have been able to break the spell. I recognized most of the pictograms from my earlier studies of the swamp witches' tome, back on Calliope, but I didn't have the knowledge necessary to stop it.

It was time to let the prince of daemons do his thing, and rid us of the last obstacle standing between me and my friends.

*Blaze, Caia, hang in there... I'm coming.*

# 18

## BLAZE

I lost track of time.

Caia and I had tried everything in this box. I'd punched at the walls. Even with her lighters taken away, I'd used my own to set a piece of fabric on fire, so she could use it on localized areas, to try to melt the meranium away. But nothing worked. We were stuck here.

I sat in a corner, while Caia rested in the opposite one, occasionally glancing at me.

"Where do you think the others are?" she asked, her voice weak. It hurt me on the inside to hear the hopelessness in her tone.

"They're probably out there somewhere, trying to find a way in, so they can get to us," I replied, unwilling to let her sink into despair.

I moved closer to her, resting my hands on her knees, and she looked up at me with glassy teal eyes.

"You're right," she breathed, her lower lip trembling slightly. "They'll be here soon..."

"It's too early to give up, Caia."

She nodded, swallowing back tears. I reached out and pulled her into my arms, holding her tight, and she rested her head against my shoulder. I kissed her hair and hummed slowly, not knowing what else to do to ease her mind.

I wasn't doing any better, either. We were both well aware that it wasn't going to be easy for Harper and the others to get to us. Not only were we trapped in a charmed meranium box, but we were surrounded by daemons, all of them eager to kill us and the rest of our team. Things didn't really look good for us, especially since I couldn't turn into a dragon without crushing Caia in this small space.

After what felt like hours, I'd gone through several emotional stages, from rage and frustration, to resignation, to an eerie sense of calm—something that felt like the quiet before a devastating storm.

She shuddered in my arms, and I realized that she was crying.

"It'll be okay, beautiful," I murmured, cupping her face with my left hand. "We'll get out of here one way or another, I promise you."

"Your optimism isn't as infectious as I'd hoped," she breathed.

I pressed my thumb under her chin, prompting her to tilt her head up and look at me. Our eyes met, and, for a brief but wonderful moment, it felt as though the world around us disappeared. For a split second in the endless fabric of time, the walls around us were gone, and all we had was each other.

Her lips parted slowly, as her gaze softened. I wondered what would happen if I kissed her. My vow of celibacy seemed fickle and useless, an obsolete nuisance. What if we weren't going to get out of here? What if the worst came to happen, and we were living out the last few days or hours of our lives?

Would I leave this world without knowing what it felt like to taste her lips?

I inched closer, ready to throw everything aside, just to feel her. My heart wrestled against my ribcage, my fire raging through me, desperate for any kind of release. Her breath hitched as I lowered my head, ready to do what I had been dreaming of for weeks.

*This is it. There's no turning back from here.*

A sharp and loud clang startled us. We both shot to our feet, flushed and breathing heavily, as if we'd just been lifting weights. I looked through the small tunnel, and the hatch door at the end opened. Zane's head popped into view. He grinned.

"Ah, I see you're still here," he quipped, adding fuel to my fire.

"Did you come here to taunt us or to help us?" I shot back. Caia came to my side. Her face lit up with hope, and I found myself praying that Zane wouldn't knock her down.

"I have very little time and no patience for silly games," Zane replied. "Your friends are here."

"Wait, what?" I yelped.

I could see the world in color again when Harper and Caspian appeared by his side. Whatever invisibility spell they had been wearing, it expired just then.

"Harper! Lord Kifo!" Caia gasped.

They both frowned, then glanced at each other.

"Okay, so that's, what... three, four hours?" Harper asked Caspian.

"Looks like it." He nodded.

"And I only had half a satchel," Harper said. She then beamed at Caia and me. "We got our hands on some invisibility spell paste from the daemons."

"You have no idea how good it is to see you!" Caia cried out, wiping more tears.

"Yeah, I've heard that one before," Harper chuckled, giving us a wink.

"Okay, you can hug and kiss later. I need to get rid of this." Zane rolled his eyes and used his claws to scratch away at the edge of the small tunnel. He muttered something, and the entire passage lit up with familiar symbols, bright orange against the meranium surface.

The charm that Shaytan had put on the box vanished.

"Now hurry, send the fae through first," Zane said.

I helped Caia up, lifting her so she could get into the

tunnel. She crawled through, and I breathed a sigh of relief when Harper and Caspian got her out.

"Okay, now do your thing, dragon." The daemon prince smirked.

They all pulled themselves back, and I used my fire breath on the meranium. I had been longing to do this for hours, and I was thrilled to watch the metal turn into an incandescent yellow blob as it melted away. In less than a minute, the front side of the meranium box was gone, and a wide path had been cleared for me to pass through. I understood then how they'd gotten me in, in the first place—they'd literally taken down one wall, then sealed it and added swamp witch charms to stop me from melting it all away.

I reunited with Harper and Caia, hugging them both and laughing with sheer joy, as if I hadn't seen them in ages. Freedom was an incredible thing to experience after being deprived of it.

"How did you make it all the way here?" Caia asked.

"We had to split into pairs, because there's another meranium box in the east wing and I can't see through the damn thing," Harper replied. "We got lucky and ran into Zane."

"He was kind enough to help us reach you," Caspian added, giving Zane an appreciative nod. "Hansa and Jax are on the other side. We're supposed to meet over in the south wing."

"Wait, if they're on the other side, checking that other

meranium box, how will they know they're in the wrong place?" I asked.

"They'd open the latch and see that the box is empty. Anyway, you can catch up once you're out of here," Zane said, reminding us that our escape was nowhere near over at this point.

Harper handed us a couple of satchels. Caia and I swallowed their contents, while Harper and Caspian did the same, then gave us two red lenses, and we watched each other disappear.

"This stuff is weaker than the original spell, but it will do," Harper replied. "We need to be careful, and not look any of the daemons in the eye. Use the lenses so we can keep track of each other as we move."

"Where are you meeting the others?" Zane asked.

"There's a totem in the south wing. I think it's the only one," Harper said.

"It is. It was a gift from the king of Imen, from thousands of years ago, long before his kind came around." The daemon prince nodded at Caspian. "It was a short-lived attempt at peace. I'll take you there. Just stick to the sides and use the statues for cover, if you need to."

One by one, we followed Zane as he guided us out of the chamber. We stepped over the dead daemon guards, careful not to step into any of the blood pools that had formed around them. It took me a while to adjust to the titanic size of the palace and everything in it—the entire place had been designed to come across as grandiose and brimming with luxury. And it did just that.

In this impressive, expansive enemy territory, I couldn't help but feel a little small. But then I quickly remembered what they had done, and how they'd managed to cage me, and my chest swelled with the eagerness to go full dragon and torch them all to hell.

Soon enough, I'd get my chance. This wasn't my last incursion into a daemon city.

I could feel it in my bones.

# 19

## HARPER

### (DAUGHTER OF HAZEL & TEJUS)

It took us another half hour or so to reach the totem in the south wing, mainly because of the frequent hiding breaks we had to take on the way there. The daemon guards were wearing their lenses, making it more difficult for us to sneak through the hallway in a straight line and forcing us to seek shelter behind statues and curtains.

"Lucky for us that Shaytan likes his fine art, huh?" Caia whispered.

We were on our own again, with Zane leading the way.

"Yes, my father loves these statues," he muttered, his discontent quite obvious. "Personally, I think they're a ghastly waste of space, but hey, I'm not in charge. Besides, he's found a new use for them. Anyway, here we are."

We gathered around the totem. It was a beautiful piece,

reaching all the way to the ceiling, with a dozen, beautifully sculpted heads stacked one on top of the other. Their gemstone eyes seemed to look down at us, amber flames reflected on their many sharp facets.

"Are these Imen? Or daemons? I'm a bit confused," I muttered, staring at the golden heads. There were sinuous lines and horns protruding from six of them, while the other six seemed normal... if normal could be defined as "not being a daemon".

"They're both. Six of our former kings, and six of theirs. They were always at war, and the totem was intended to bring them together, to symbolize peace," Zane explained. "Then my grandfather went ahead and ruined it. The truce lasted for exactly six months."

A couple of minutes passed as we kept a lookout. Then Hansa and Jax emerged from the west wing, and stilled at the sight of Zane.

"We're good," I said, noticing they had red lenses on, as well. "Zane's here to help us."

"Ah, so you're the infamous Zane." Hansa pursed her lips.

"I take it my name's come up in your conversations?" Zane raised an eyebrow, taking off his red lens to clean it.

"You could say that," I shot back. "Not sure you remember, but you kidnapped my friend?"

"Oh. Yeah." He chuckled, one hand resting on his long knife handle, which was mounted on his leather belt. "Good times."

"I guess we should thank you?" Jax replied with a slight frown. Hansa lit up when she saw Caia and Blaze behind us.

"Oh, my darlings!" she croaked, and rushed to hug them both, then glanced at Caspian and me. "Let's get out of here. We have so much news!"

"Yeah, tell me about it." I snorted. "We just paid a visit to the king's harem."

"We saw Darius. Alive," Jax replied bluntly, and I froze, unable to process that snippet of information.

"Um, what now?" I managed, feeling as if my brain were glitching.

"Uh oh." Zane's low voice interrupted us.

We all followed his gaze to find one of his brothers—a prince, to be specific—staring at us through his red lens from across the eastern hallway. Heat burst through me as my instincts kicked in. Hansa cursed under her breath, and I heard the screech of her broadsword leaving its scabbard.

"Brother?" the daemon prince murmured. "I thought I'd heard your voice just now. What the hell are you doing?"

"Cayn," Zane replied, his lens still off as he stared at his brother. "I'm just... thinking out loud. Long day. Why?"

"The outsiders! They've got you surrounded!" Cayn growled and drew his sword, coming right at us. I pushed a strong barrier out, knocking him back. He landed on the stone floor with a heavy thud, twenty yards away from us, groaning from the pain.

"What? Really? I hadn't noticed," Zane replied dryly, then

put on his lens and looked at me, lowering his voice as he briefly nodded behind Caspian and me. "Go all the way to the end, down the stairs, and out through the service door. It's right at the bottom of the stairs. Follow that path; it will lead you to the back of the palace and onto the belt road. You'll see three tunnels opening on the west side. The one in the middle will take you straight into the western plains. Now, go!"

I nodded, and Hansa, Jax, Blaze, and Caia moved behind me. Zane gave me a brief wink.

"Sorry about this," he whispered, then raised his voice, feigning outrage. "You! You fiends! I've got you now!"

He drew his knife and slashed at me, while his brother came back to his senses and jumped to his feet. We ran to the end of the hallway, and Zane and Cayn came after us.

"You heard him," I breathed as we darted across the black stone floor, the stairs just thirty yards ahead. Loud horns blared all around us, and I briefly glanced over my shoulder to see Cayn blowing into a dark blue crystal.

"Swamp witch magic," Jax said, as he followed my gaze.

I cursed under my breath and picked up speed, with Caspian close by my side.

Hatches opened in the ceiling above. Water poured down from them and splashed us, compromising our invisibility spells and making us all too visible. My blood ran cold.

A flurry of footsteps and growls erupted behind us. Daemon soldiers poured in from both the east and west wings, joining Cayn and Zane as they chased after us, their weapons drawn and fangs bared. I would've been perfectly happy just with that increasing mass of soul-eating fiends headed our way, but my pulse quickened when several massive pit wolf statues rippled and became *real*, joining the chase.

"Oh, crap," I muttered. Ear-piercing shrieks echoed through the hallway, curdling my blood, as statues of death claws came to life as well, and flew after us. "Crap! Crap! Crap!" I shouted. "He didn't say anything about the statues coming to life!"

"I think this is what he meant by 'new use for them', the vague bastard," Caspian hissed.

We shot down the stairs, leaping down full flights at a time. My heart was throbbing, and adrenaline was coursing through me, my entire body shifting into survival mode.

This was it. Our grand dash to freedom.

# 20

---

## JAX

As we flew down the stairs, a horde of daemons poured from the main hallway, joined by massive pit wolves and death claws that had materialized from obsidian statues. We drew our swords, our instincts already sharpened by previous encounters with the creatures.

My senses flared as we reached the ground floor, the daemons closing in on us.

The death claws' shrieks scratched my brain, tightening my muscles as I followed Harper toward the service exit that Zane had mentioned. She looked over her shoulder at us, then farther back, before she put her hand out.

"Move aside!"

We shifted to the left and right, and she pushed out a barrier and knocked back the first few rows of daemons

coming after us. I knew it wasn't going to be enough, so I
slowed down a little, joined by Hansa and Caia—they quickly
caught on, understanding what I wanted to do. I always
carried lighters in case Caia ever lost hers, so I fished two from
my back pocket and tossed them over to her.

"We need to get out, now!" Blaze shouted.

I slashed my swords at the first daemons that reached us,
drawing rich spurts of crimson blood. Hansa did the same,
hacking at the creatures, while Caia flipped her lighters open
and shot bright balls of fire at two pit wolves.

We managed to push them back by several feet, before the
death claws swooped down. We ducked, then raced after
Harper and the others as they burst through the service door.

"Let's go!" I barked, then shoved one sword through the
chest of a daemon, kicking him so he landed back against the
others.

We made it to the courtyard, which was wide enough for
what could turn into a deadly fight for us. I could see the belt
road ahead, approximately two hundred yards away. I ran fast,
with Hansa close by my side. Caia was not far behind, sending
fireballs over her shoulder and making it increasingly difficult
for the daemons to get to us.

"Out of my way!" Blaze growled.

We all did as instructed and spread out, as he turned full
dragon. I could never get over his majestic size, the amber-
orange scales on his belly reminding me of what devastating
fire burned in his throat.

The death claws flew around, trying to circle him, while the daemons seemed to waiver, as did the pit wolves, not sure whether they should move ahead and keep attacking us. I saw the princes, all seven of them, along with several giant generals, at the far end of the crowd. Fear widened their red eyes, but something told me they weren't going to give up that easily.

Blaze, however, didn't give a damn. He positioned himself between us and the daemons, leaving very few of them brave enough to sneak past him and come at us. He swatted away at the death claws with the single spikes on the tips of his wings and his tail, knocking the creatures down. They hit the hard ground, and only a couple managed to get back up, while the others were left looking like crumpled pieces of paper.

He stomped and thrashed around, crushing daemons by the dozens. I could hear their bones snapping and their screams of horror as he brought his jaws down and chewed on them like they were candy—breaking them between his fangs.

It made it a whole lot easier for us to fight back. Soon enough, Blaze started to spit fire, engulfing the thinning crowd of daemons in bright orange flames. They screamed and wailed as they desperately tried to get away, but Blaze wasn't done yet. His long neck shuddered, and he released another obliterating heatwave, forcing the princes to step back and keep their distance.

The alarms were sounding all over the city, and I could hear more daemons coming in—not just from the palace, but also from the surrounding areas. Soon enough, the enemies could end up outnumbering us, even with a dragon on our side.

# 21

## HANSA

Blaze was relentless. He continued to decimate the armed forces of daemons, while Jax, Caia, Harper, Caspian, and I fought the bold dozen who had managed to avoid the dragon's fiery breath. More death claws were coming in from the city, and I could hear the pit wolves growling as they snuck in from the belt road.

Daemons roared through the neighboring streets as they made their way to the palace. The alarms were blaring, loud horns calling the people to take up arms and come get us.

I dodged a hit from a rapier and brought my sword out to the side in response, lodging the blade deep into a daemon's hip. It cried out from the pain as I jerked my sword hand and executed a three-hundred-and-sixty-degree turn and cut the creature's head off with one swift blow.

We'd made it this far, and there was no way in hell that I

was letting these horned bastards get the best of me or my people. I roared as I thrust my broadsword right through the spine of another daemon, just as he was preparing to pounce on Caia from behind. The crunching of steel cutting through bone made my blood rush, and I pulled my sword out and moved on to the next soldier.

I got rid of him quickly, but the glimmer of light reflected on a curved blade slashing toward me caught my eye. A split second later, I'd already jumped back to get a better look at my opponent. My heart jolted as I realized that I was facing a prince. Somehow, this oversized lump of muscles and golden armor had made his way down to us.

He carried two rapiers, which he brought down repeatedly with swift and effortless movements. I blocked most of his hits, and dodged others, before bringing my broadsword up at a forty-five-degree angle in an attempt to get his chest and throat. I missed him by inches, and nearly paid the price with my life, as one of his rapiers came hard from the left. I tilted my head back so the blade wouldn't remove my head from my shoulders.

My ears rang from a sharp clang, and I saw Jax's blades intervene, blocking another of the prince's hits.

"You're not getting away, little mice!" the prince sneered, relentless in his attacks.

"You sound just like your father, and trust me when I say that's not a good thing," I shot back, and managed to cut through his shoulder. He hissed from the pain, but didn't get a chance to respond, as Jax slashed at his hip, before Harper knocked him back with a barrier. It wasn't enough to kill him, but it helped a lot.

It was the small window we needed to fall back, as more daemons were starting to pour through from both the palace and the nearby streets.

Blaze roared, then rained down a curtain of fire, covering the land around him in orange flames and screams of agony, while we all made our way toward the belt road. Once we reached it, our chances of survival would increase substantially, leaving only about fifty feet between us and the tunnel leading out to the western plains.

# 22

---

## CAIA

### (DAUGHTER OF GRACE & LAWRENCE)

I gave Blaze all the backup I could provide, targeting mostly pit wolves that had managed to sneak past the flames, and the death claws flying overhead. They knew that his eyes were his weak spot, so I had to make sure that they got nowhere near them.

Harper and the others kept daemons away as we tried to move back and head for the belt road. Fireballs were the easiest for me to shoot out, particularly where the death claws were involved, but the pit wolves were becoming more difficult to handle.

Two of them came at me simultaneously, prompting me to shoot out fireballs with one hand and raise a thin curtain of fire with the other, but it wasn't enough. Sooner or later, the beasts would find a way to go around that and get to me.

It was time for something more drastic, as Blaze was left with only a couple of death claws to deal with at this point, while spitting tidal waves of fire over the daemons coming in from the palace. I summoned all the energy I had, allowing my body to channel it all into my hands. I brought them together, lighters in the middle.

I'd only tried it a few times before—my last attempt had been with Vita, back on Calliope, but I had to give it another push, so I did my best to fashion a large broadsword made of pure fire. It needed to be strong and concentrated enough for it to work like an actual blade.

The fire curtain in front of me was beginning to fade, and the pit wolves were snapping their jaws at me, shuddering with excitement. They knew they could soon attack. There was no time to waiver. No room for mistakes. I grunted, giving myself one last push, then gasped as my sword gained its full, incandescent form.

One of the pit wolves got ahead of itself and charged me. I brought my flame sword up, aiming straight forward at the pit wolf's charmed collar. The fire blade cut through it, and the beast stilled, its red eyes blinking as the swamp witch magic faded. It was no longer under the control of daemons. It had a mind of its own again, and it didn't want to fight me.

When the second pit wolf came at me, I lifted my flaming sword again, ready to cut its collar off and free it, but the first creature intervened and tackled it. They fought for a while, until the second wolf's collar snapped off and hit the ground.

It froze, its red eyes wide. It yelped at its companion, and they both looked at me, then started attacking the daemons slipping past Blaze's flames.

All of a sudden, we had two creatures on our side, sinking their incredibly sharp fangs into the soldiers' throats. They were perfectly capable of breaking the iron of charmed collars; daemon throats were much softer and easier to shred.

Other daemons came at me, and I blocked a couple of their hits, before slashing at them with my incandescent sword. It cut through so fast, so unforgivingly, that they fell to the ground in pieces, the smell of burnt flesh filling my nostrils. Those behind them realized what I was holding, and didn't seem too eager to attack me anymore.

This was a weapon made entirely from fire. With enough energy in it to cut like high-intensity lasers, the daemons didn't stand a chance against it. Against me.

"Fall back," I heard Jax shout from behind.

I looked up, watching Blaze as he rammed his jaws into the thinning crowd of daemons, before he let out another round of scorching fire. Harper, Caspian, Jax, and Hansa were already moving away, cutting down anyone who stood between us and the belt road just fifty yards ahead.

It was time to make a run for it, as I could see the tunnel we needed to get through.

Our way out.

# 23

## HARPER

### (DAUGHTER OF HAZEL & TEJUS)

My energy levels were running a little low, but I still had plenty in me to fight my way out of here. I'd used a succession of barriers and sword attacks to strike down dozens of daemons. Blaze had successfully held Shaytan's soldiers back, burning most of them to a crisp.

There were more coming in from the city, and I could hear the screeching of death claws in the distance. We couldn't stay here anymore. If we kept on fighting, we would soon be outnumbered again, and I feared that Shaytan himself would join the scuffle—and none of us were in any way prepared for him.

Blaze started to move back as well, while we made a run for it, and headed toward the belt road. I dashed forward and slipped into the tunnel that Zane had told me about. He was still somewhere on the other side of the courtyard, with his brothers, who were probably wondering whether they would get killed if they came after us. They were already watching hundreds of their soldiers burn before Blaze—surely, they had some sense in them.

Everything happened extremely fast from there on. I ran up through the tunnel, followed closely by Jax, Caspian, Hansa, and Caia. Blaze quickly shifted and joined us. Caia sent fireballs down at the daemons coming after us. It was a narrow space, and they had nowhere to go to avoid the flames.

I heard their bones crackling like logs in a campfire, along with their screams of agony, as I kept moving forward. I could see the light at the end, and that gave me the push I needed to run faster and climb up to the surface.

The sun was out, so I immediately pulled my hood over my head to shield my face.

"Cover yourselves up," I shouted over my shoulder, then turned around.

One by one, the rest of my team came out. There were three tunnel openings in front of me, the one in the middle, through which we'd just come, and the other two on either side, with twenty feet of limestone between them.

I summoned all the energy I could find and pushed out a barrier through each tunnel, enough to cause them to collapse. The daemons that were coming through all three were crushed, and I could hear them crying out as chunks of limestone rumbled and sealed off the passageways.

We looked around, realizing that we had exited into the opening of the gorge, and we could see the western plains stretching ahead, their waves of green grass and thick forests waiting for us.

The ground beneath trembled, not just from the collapse of the three tunnels, but also from the hundreds of daemons pouring in from farther inside the gorge. We could see them, little black dots getting bigger as they ran toward us, their weapons drawn and their fangs bared.

"We have to hold them back," Jax breathed.

"I'll handle it," a very naked Blaze replied, then shifted back to full dragon form and started lashing a spiked tail at the gorge walls. Large chunks of dark gray stone crashed into the middle of the ravine, and Blaze used his jaws as well, chipping away at the walls and hurling rocks from both sides. The obstruction grew bigger. He climbed on top of the giant mound and spat more fire at the daemons coming in, enough to burn them alive and keep the others away.

He continued to break down pieces of the wall, until the entire portion of the gorge was blocked, permanently sealed, giving us the window we needed to run out into the western plains.

"Holy crap," Hansa gasped. "We actually made it!"

"Last one to reach the plains is a stinky Sluagh!" I grinned.

I darted out of the gorge, with Hansa, Caspian, Jax, Caia, and Blaze hot on my trail.

Seemingly endless fields of green opened out before us,

and our feet sank into the tall grass. We ran as fast as we could, while the daemons were left behind, beyond sealed tunnels and the crumbled ravine.

They were going to come after us, sooner or later. But, for the time being, we'd made it, and we could find a spot in the shade somewhere, catch our breaths, and regroup.

Judging by the suns' positions in the sky, it was shortly before noon when we reached the first patch of woods. I was the first one to stop beneath a giant tree and lie down, breathing in and out, as I relished the taste of freedom on the tip of my tongue.

## 24

## CAIA

### (DAUGHTER OF GRACE & LAWRENCE)

B laze slipped into a pair of pants, one of the several that the team carried in their backpacks. We'd lost ours when we were captured. We settled in the shade of a large tree, a couple of miles away from the gorge we'd just collapsed.

It took us a while to simply refocus on what we had to do, while we all enjoyed the fresh air and just being back on the surface, out of that meranium box, and out of that damn city.

"I think we killed at least six, maybe eight hundred of their soldiers back there," Jax said.

"You might want to add the ones who didn't make it out of the tunnels, and the ones I burned back inside the gorge," Blaze added, running a hand through his dark hair.

"How many do you think we took out, in the end?" I replied.

Something had changed in the way Blaze was looking at me. It must've had something to do with our moment back in the meranium cage. I mean, we'd almost kissed. There was a peculiar warmth in his midnight-blue eyes, much more intense and specifically aimed at me. It made my heart flutter, but all I could do was exhale sharply and save that thought for later.

"I'd say at least twelve, even thirteen hundred." Blaze grinned.

"We need a new action plan," Harper said, her brow furrowed. "What was that about Darius, Hansa?"

"Yeah, please do expand on that," I chimed in.

"There isn't much for me to tell you, other than the fact that both Jax and I saw Darius, very much alive and kicking, in Shaytan's throne room," Hansa replied. "His death was staged. And I think it's safe to assume that so were the explosions. He snuck out of the city and met with the king of daemons. I think they're in cahoots, somehow."

"I'm not sure if the others know—I mean, the other Maras," Jax added, then looked at Caspian. "Do your people know, Lord Kifo?"

We all stared at Caspian for a while, but his expression was firm and didn't give anything away.

"Is there something you're not telling us?" Harper asked.

He gave her a pained look, nervously scratching the back of his head. "I wish I could tell you more, but honestly, I can't. But the rogue Imen can help you with this."

"Dammit, Lord Kifo," Hansa growled, while Harper cursed under her breath. "After all we've been through so far, you still don't trust us? It's ridiculous."

"It's not even about trusting *us* anymore. It's the fact that you're withholding information from us," Harper said, visibly frustrated. "Information that could save our lives!"

"I'm sorry..." Caspian breathed, his gaze fixed on the grass at his feet.

"What could Darius possibly be doing with Shaytan?" I asked. Clearly, Caspian wasn't going to tell us anything else, but that didn't mean we couldn't speculate and draw several potential scenarios for us to move forward.

The rest of our team was still back in Azure Heights, and they didn't know anything about this.

"I don't know... They're supposed to be enemies, with daemons kidnapping Maras and eating their souls and all that," Hansa scoffed. "Either way, there is clearly some kind of conspiracy going on here. Darius faked his own death and seems to be good friends with the king of daemons."

"Whatever it is they're planning, they want to make sure that we don't make it back to Azure Heights and warn the others. And that is exactly what we need to do," Jax said.

"But we also need to find the rogue Imen," Harper replied. "We were already planning to do that, and you all heard Lord Kifo. They have answers. Answers we desperately need right now."

A couple of minutes went by as Jax and Hansa thought

things over. Was it just Darius who had planned this? "Do you really think the other Maras are involved? After all, a lot of innocent people died during those attacks," I muttered.

"I find it hard to believe that the Lords would willingly kill so many of their own, just to stage an explosion for Darius to get out of there. Let's not forget that there was a second explosive charge in Lord Kifo's house. If it had just been about Darius, and his faked death, I'm sure it would've been just his mansion turned to ashes," Blaze offered. "It just doesn't make sense."

"Blaze, Caia," Jax said, "you two should fly back to the city and warn the rest of our team. After that, you should summon the Lords and tell them about Darius. Watch their reactions carefully: one of them might flinch or falter, if they were behind all this. Hell, if we're not supposed to get back there in one piece, then surely they won't be happy to see the two of you there. And should you get a whiff of danger, even the slightest hint, I need you all to pack up and come to this area. Avril will be capable enough of tracking us to wherever the rogue tribe is."

"Then what will you do? Look for the Imen?" I replied.

Jax, Hansa, and Harper looked at each other, then nodded.

"You heard Lord Kifo." Jax smirked. "He obviously knows more than he's telling us, but something stops him from talking, so he'll be kind enough to take us to the tribe. We need to get to the truth, as soon as possible, before more innocent people disappear and die."

"That makes sense," Blaze said, then stood up and took his pants off. My cheeks caught fire. The others instantly looked away, visibly embarrassed. I covered my eyes, all flushed.

"Dude, some warning would've been nice!" Harper snapped.

Blaze pushed the pants into my hands, while I kept my eyes tightly shut. "Sorry about that, but it's not like we have dozens of clothes just lying around for me to put on whenever I shift. Might as well hold onto these until we get back to Azure Heights."

I heard his footsteps through the grass, then the familiar shuffle of his body, his bones cracking as he turned back into a dragon. I opened my eyes and found him standing beyond the tree shade, his wings stretching as he looked at me.

"Be careful out there," Hansa said. We both got up, and she hugged me. "If everything is okay back in the city, wait for us there. Obviously, if it isn't, do as Jax said. And take these."

She gave me two red lenses, which I slipped into the chest pocket of my leather suit. "We will have to make do with these, for now." I nodded. "But as soon as we get a chance, we'll look through the city for red garnet so our entire team can carry one."

"Fly safe." Harper took me in her arms. "And burn down every single one of them if they try to hurt you or capture you again."

"Don't worry, Cuz, I'll give them hell." I winked, then walked over to Blaze.

He lowered himself so I could climb up onto his back, gripping the thick scales over his shoulders as he took flight. We soared into the blue sky. My hair was loose, fluttering in the wind as I looked down and watched the world get smaller with every second.

I worried about Harper and the others. I even worried about Caspian. Despite his secrecy, he'd helped us. He'd put his life at risk for us. There must've been a solid, valid reason for why he couldn't tell us the whole truth. Knowing Harper, she was bound to get to the bottom of it, one way or another.

In the meantime, however, I held onto Blaze's back as we flew over the gorges, heading straight for the mountain. He glided farther to the right so that whatever daemons were left in the ravine wouldn't see us.

The thought of the other Maras knowing about Darius put Avril, Fiona, Scarlett, Heron, and Patrik at risk. I'd already seen the inside of a meranium box. There was no way I was going to let my friends experience that fear and hopelessness.

# 25

## HARPER

### (DAUGHTER OF HAZEL & TEJUS)

Twenty minutes later, we were trekking through the deep woods that sprawled over the western plains. Trees as tall as giants, with thick, straight trunks, rose around us, the rich overhead foliage keeping the sun out. Birds trilled from the branches above, a variety of high notes that made me feel like I was in the better part of a grim tale.

Deer-like creatures watched us from a distance as I used my True Sight to look for signs of Imen tribes. Caspian walked closely by my side, while Jax and Hansa stayed behind, covering our backs.

The silence weighed heavy on my shoulders, the tension between Caspian and me almost palpable. I was conflicted, mainly because I couldn't trust Caspian—not fully, anyway, as he was clearly not telling us everything. I didn't understand why, and he wasn't going to tell me either, so I was left in a state of limbo that ate away at me.

"Try farther to the northwest," Caspian suggested, his voice low.

"Have you been in these parts before?" I asked.

"Not for the last couple of years," he replied. "But they should be here somewhere. They're far enough from the gorge, on this side. I doubt they would go any farther. Some of them hold hope that their brethren back in Azure Heights will eventually change their minds, and will come here, looking for the Free People."

I didn't have anything to say to that, as my mind kept wandering back to wondering why he wasn't telling us the whole truth. It nagged at me, like a dull migraine.

"I just can't understand how you could continue to with-hold information like this!" I finally burst out. "Whatever oath you swore, how does it still hold validity when one of your own, Darius—a leader and supposedly an example of high morals—has betrayed everyone by aligning himself with Shay-tan, the freaking king of daemons? How?"

A minute passed quietly. I glanced at Caspian. He seemed genuinely remorseful, and yet he still wasn't helping. And that made me angry in ways I had never experienced before, mainly because I expected more of him—I had feelings for him, and I couldn't see myself falling for someone who didn't stand for doing the right thing no matter what. His elusiveness went against my own set of ethics, and was in direct contrast with what my heart wanted from him.

"I can't really explain why I can't tell you everything," he replied, and I caught a tremor in his voice, a weakness that hadn't been there before. "But someday I will, with my own words. But until then, I promise you, Miss Hellswan, that I will do everything in my power to help you and your team bring all those responsible for so much death... to justice. I swear it upon my life."

We gazed at each other for a while, lost in our thoughts.

Everything he'd displayed so far felt genuine. It felt true. Something was actively stopping him from talking about the daemons, about Darius, and about what went on in Azure Heights. And besides, I wanted to believe him. I wanted to trust him.

A twig broke under a foot, thirty feet to my left. I heard a bow stretching, and I stilled, lifting an arm to signal the others to stop.

"One move, and you all die," a raspy feminine voice shot through the woods.

I turned my head to see Vesta, the young water fae who had helped us the other day, back in the gorge. She was joined by ten Imen, and they all wore the same patches of brown leather, tightly fastened around their trunks, hips, and calves with black strings. Orange dots were painted on their temples, making me think that they might be some kind of tribal status symbol.

They all aimed their arrows at us, and I could see that the sharp metal tips had been dipped in a purple fluid. Something told me it was going to hurt like hell if they shot us with them.

"Vesta, we meet again," I said politely, keeping my tone calm and even, and my hands up. I slowly shifted my body to the side so I could face her.

"What are you doing here?" she asked, frowning, pulling her arrow farther back just to show us that she wasn't kidding.

"We've been looking for you," I replied. "We need your help."

She measured me from head to toe, then looked at Jax and Hansa, and I noticed the glimmer of recognition in her blue eyes. She then frowned when she moved her gaze to Caspian.

"What is he doing here? Why did you bring him here?" she hissed, clearly unhappy to see him. That just made me want to ask more questions, as I was beginning to think that they already knew each other. I'd seen her expression back in the gorge, but I had chalked it up to mere wariness of his species in general, and not specific dislike.

"There was an attack in Azure Heights. Innocent people died, Maras and Imen alike," I said. "We then went into the daemon city beneath the gorge to scope out the enemy... and we have a lot of questions for you, the Free People, in particular. We couldn't get our answers from Azure Heights, and the daemons will come looking for us soon. We need your help, Vesta. You have to tell us what's going on in this world."

She seemed to think about it for a few seconds, then nodded at Caspian.

"I may know a couple of things, but our elders can better answer any questions you might have," she replied. "But I'm not telling you or showing you anything until Lord Kifo is restrained and blindfolded. And that is just a courtesy I'm extending, because our orders are to kill him, and any other Mara from Azure Heights, on sight."

"I don't get it." I shook my head. "What's your deal with him? He's here with us. He's helping us. He's risking his life for us. Lord Kifo is not the enemy."

"You're clearly not from around here." Vesta raised an eyebrow. Two of her Imen put their bows away and took out pieces of string and a wide strip of fabric from their bags, stepping forward. "You don't get to decide who the enemy is. Even I don't get to decide who the enemy is. Only the elders. So, if you want to speak to them, you have to follow our rules."

"It's okay, Miss Hellswan," Caspian interjected. Our eyes met, and he gave me a brief, warm smile as he put his hands out. "Let them bind me however they see fit. I will not resist."

"Listen, I know we didn't get off on the right foot here, clashing from the very beginning, but I'm not letting you get hurt or restrained in any way until we figure out what the hell is going on here," I replied.

He moved closer, enough for me to feel his warm breath tickling my face. "It's okay, Harper. If you can't trust me on anything else, you can at least trust me on this. I'll be fine. You need to meet the elders, and this is the price we must pay. I don't mind."

I sighed, then moved back so the Imen could do their jobs. One of them tied Caspian's hands behind his back, while the other put a blindfold over his eyes. They then nudged him, making him walk toward Vesta. Jax, Hansa, and I followed.

"Much better." Vesta winked, her lips stretching into a smile. What a contrast that was, from the fearful and almost feral fae who had joined our fight against daemons a couple of days back. "I can now take you to my people."

"I still don't get why you're so against Lord Kifo. He's obviously here to help, for Pete's sake," I groaned, increasingly frustrated. There was something about Caspian tied up like that—it just put me on edge. I hated it.

"You will soon understand why," Caspian replied.

"Rest assured, Lord Kifo, I will let the elders know of your cooperation, and make sure that no harm comes to you," Vesta said, then led the way deeper into the woods.

I was going to have to siphon some energy soon, as I used the last ounces on my True Sight, scanning the areas ahead. The tribe was there, less than a mile away, nestled between jagged rocks and giant trees.

There were hundreds of Imen moving around clay huts and conical tents. Fire burned in the middle, eating away at a pile of dry wood. I glanced over my shoulder at Hansa and Jax, and they both gave me a reassuring nod. We continued our walk.

Even they had noticed how uncomfortable I was.

However, I had to admit, Caspian was right. Having him bound and blindfolded was a small price to pay for the truth that we were going to get. Finally, after what seemed like forever, we were going to find out what was going on here, on Neraka, with the daemons, the Maras, and the Imen.

Clearly, the people in Azure Heights either didn't know everything, or had expertly lied to us. And for their sake, I hoped the former was the case.

# 26

## CAIA

(DAUGHTER OF GRACE & LAWRENCE)

Blaze glided over the Valley of Screams, and I held on and welcomed the cool high-altitude air brushing through my hair and filling my lungs.

I occasionally glanced below, noticing shadows as they darted through the ravines. I couldn't see very well from this height, but I felt as though it was safe to assume that those were daemons, maybe following us from afar.

What might their plan be, though? Surely they weren't crazy enough to try to attack us, not when Blaze was in full dragon form. They kept to the shade, hiding beneath the trees, before they shot forward.

"We've definitely dealt a big blow to the daemons, especially inside their city," I said, mostly to myself, but also to Blaze. "With so many of them dead, they will probably need time to recover. Some are following us now, but I'm not sure what their aim is."

"They'll probably have to report back to Shaytan," Blaze's gruff voice came through, as his massive wings flapped.

"Yeah, it's not like they can do anything else at this point," I replied. "Besides, I don't think we have more than one, maybe two days before reinforcements arrive from other daemon cities. You heard Mose, there are plenty of other daemons ready to take up arms against us."

"For now, we just need to find out if the Lords knew about Darius," he grumbled.

He was right. What Darius had done was beyond comprehension, and definitely beyond forgiveness. My mind kept going back to Rewa, and the seemingly endless stream of tears that she'd cried when she had recognized her father's Lordship ring... and when they had cremated what were supposed to be his remains.

Her grief couldn't possibly have been made up. That pain, it had to be real. I just couldn't imagine someone so perfectly capable of such deceit. Frankly, I wasn't too crazy about her, mainly because of the way in which she kept approaching Blaze, but that was just my jealousy rearing its ugly head.

And what about the others? Members of the other Lords' families had perished in those fires. Dozens of innocent Imen were also gone. No, it just didn't make sense. Darius must have made some kind of deal with the daemons. He must have switched sides, taking many of his own down in the process.

And he'd specifically targeted Lord Kifo, too. Maybe Caspian knew something. Maybe he'd suspected something about Darius and his intentions. Maybe he'd even confronted him, prompting Darius to rig the Kifo mansion with explosives as well.

After all, Caspian was out here, with us. He was putting his life at risk to help us. No way was he involved in whatever Darius had put together with Shaytan. But even looking at it from afar, even as I tried to visualize the full picture, there were still blanks in desperate need of filling in, in order for me to really understand what this was all about.

On one hand, we had daemons organized in underground cities, rallying their armies as they hunted innocent creatures for their souls. On the other, we had a mountain city where Imen and Maras had supposedly learned to coexist in peace and harmony—but something rotten lay underneath, secrets untold, strange behaviors, and an alarming amount of mind-bending. It just didn't seem right.

And then, way beyond the gorges that sealed Azure Heights away from the rest of the continent, were the Free People, the rogue Imen, who wanted nothing to do with the Maras, while they struggled to keep their own safe from the daemons.

We were smack in the middle of it, with the king of daemons eager to capture us and eat our souls, making us sound like some kind of... exotic delicacy. The planet wasn't kind to us either, preventing us from reaching out to Calliope, to our GASP base and our families. We couldn't even leave Neraka.

It seemed as though the deeper we dug, the more filth we uncovered.

About twenty miles ahead, the eastern plains stretched in deep shades of green, with narrow tributary streams snaking across. The deep blue ocean stretched endlessly to our right, while the mountain rose proudly beyond the field.

I could make out the shapes of Azure Heights, the streets and terraces, and hundreds of white marble buildings with reddish rooftops. The mountain ridges were dressed in deep velvet green, thick woods bordering the city. And within those white marble walls were secrets—which I yearned to uncover.

Whatever they were hiding, whether it had anything to do with Darius and the daemons or not, we were going to get to the bottom of it all. I'd lost my patience. I wanted to get out of here. I wanted to be back on Calliope, getting to know Blaze better and training with my sister and best friends.

No more of this...

No more running for our lives. We were members of GASP. We were supposed to be the ones restoring law and order, and protecting those who couldn't defend themselves. We weren't supposed to be the victims, not in this world, and not in any other.

# 27

## AVRIL

### (DAUGHTER OF LUCAS & MARION)

We met back at the infirmary as soon as the afternoon settled in shades of orange and deep pink across the sky. Our forays into the city had not yielded as many results as we had wanted.

"Imen keep collapsing in the city," Patrik concluded after both Fiona and I shared our accounts of slumber before death cases that we'd encountered. "I'm guessing no one was able to tell you much about the illness and how it manifests?"

"Not really, no." Heron shook his head. "We haven't learned anything new regarding symptoms, but, based on what Avril and I saw, the Imen literally wither away past a certain age. It's not absolute, though. There are some elders in the city, still, but the majority seem to gradually slip into this... slumber before death state."

"They brought them to the infirmary," I said. "We could talk to them later, maybe? If they're awake, that is."

"You could, yes." Patrik nodded slowly, then gazed out the window. "Another hour or two and I'll be able to try something with that asteroid belt. Maybe we can restore Telluris communications with Calliope. Judging by how things have been going for us so far, it's a big 'maybe'."

"No, no," Scarlett replied, a brief smile crossing her face, "you're supposed to be the energetic optimist in this group, Patrik. The universe won't flow your way if you go into it half-hearted, and you know it."

Patrik's gaze softened on her for a moment, before he looked at us. Something had shifted between them, and I looked forward to the end of this Neraka nonsense, so I could drill Scarlett for answers. We had grown up together; we told each other everything. If she was getting into a relationship with the Druid, I was supposed to know about it. I was going to tell her about my internal struggles regarding Heron, too. As soon as we had a moment to ourselves.

But I had to set those thoughts aside for the time being. There was an overall feeling of uneasiness dangling between us. Heron let out a long sigh, leaning against the wall behind him. I'd never seen him so disheartened before.

"Nothing seems real," he muttered. "Everything in this damn city feels... off. It's like... It's like we can see everything and everyone, but I just can't shake this feeling that something is... I don't know, *foul*."

"I feel you," Patrik replied, a glimmer of sympathy in his eyes. "We're all seeing a very pretty picture, and evil daemons trying to destroy it, but the closer we look at the picture itself, the more the rot beneath starts to show."

"I honestly cannot wait to get out of here," Scarlett murmured.

"As soon as we find a way off the planet," I said, frowning. "Neraka doesn't want us to leave yet."

"Neraka doesn't want us to do a lot of things, apparently," Heron added, and our gazes locked for a few seconds, before he shifted his focus to Patrik. "Harper and the others should be back by midnight, but if they aren't, do we all go after them?"

"Let's hope it doesn't come to that, but yes." Patrik nodded.

A spine-tingling growl came from outside, along with the sound of large wings flapping. I recognized that combination immediately and rushed to the window. Blaze had just landed outside the infirmary, with Caia on his back.

"They're back!" Scarlett exclaimed from my side. "Wait..."

"Where are the others?" Patrik muttered, his brow furrowed.

We watched as Caia got off Blaze, then handed him a pair of pants to slip into, as he shifted back to his gorgeous, naked self. I mentally reprimanded myself for finding her beau so hot, but hey, I was only looking. I had a feeling all the girls on our team felt the same.

They came inside the infirmary, and Scarlett closed the door behind them.

"Sorry, we wanted to get back sooner rather than later," Caia said. "Some crazy stuff went down."

"Don't skimp on the details," I replied, then handed them both some water, along with some food we'd grabbed from the Broken Bow Inn on our way back from the upper levels of the city, specifically for them.


We all listened as Blaze and Caia told us about their incursion into the gorges and the underground daemon city. As per my request, they didn't leave any details out. By the end of their account, we had a clear picture of what the daemon society was like.

We learned about Shaytan, the Seven Princes, the giant generals, and the armies. We had Scarlett's pit wolf theory confirmed, too—the creatures were enslaved with the help of those charmed collars. We learned about Mose and the impending uprising of daemon pacifists; they could be potential allies, and given how desperately we needed someone on the inside, reaching out to them seemed like the next logical step.

They told us about the death claws and the meranium boxes, their abduction and Darius. That was when we all froze, gawking at Blaze and Caia for a couple of minutes, until it all sank in.

"You've got to be kidding me," I gasped.

"Nope, Hansa and Jax saw and heard him clearly." Caia shook her head slowly. "He's got some plans, and they depend exclusively on our capture. They didn't want us back here in the city, for some reason. They went to a lot of trouble to keep us underground, but... you know... dragon."

She smirked as she nodded toward Blaze, who offered a shy shrug in return.

"We made our way out of there in the end," he added. "Collapsed some of their tunnels and sealed off one of the gorges, just to keep them back. I estimate somewhere between twelve and fifteen hundred casualties on their side."

Fiona and I then briefed Caia and Blaze on everything we'd learned on our side, from the collapsing Imen to our brief encounter with Cadmus, and Fiona's encounters with Zane from the night before.

"Speaking of which, Zane helped us," Caia said, looking at Fiona, whose eyes widened with surprise. "Harper and Caspian convinced him to help get us out. One of his brothers stumbled upon us as we planned our exit. He had to pretend to try to capture us, but pointed us to the right tunnel. That's when the madness ensued, but Blaze was more than eager to repay the daemons in kind for what they had done, so... lots of fire."

"We reached the western plains, and that's where we split up," Blaze explained. "Harper and the others went looking for the rogue Imen tribes, and we came back to tell you... well, everything."

A couple of minutes went by as it all sank in. Once more, dozens of questions surfaced in the back of my head, and barely a handful of possible answers.

"So, let me get this straight." Patrik attempted to draw a conclusion. "Darius faked his own death, killing dozens of Imen and even some of the Lords' family members in the process, as part of some alliance he's got with Shaytan, the king of daemons?"

"It looks like it, yes." Caia nodded.

"Do the other Maras know?" he replied, a muscle twitching in his jaw.

"We're not sure. Caspian couldn't tell us. He's under some kind of oath, and he just flat-out refused to confirm or deny, but we can't fully fault him for that. He's been with us, risking his life for us, and, most importantly, he's now helping Harper reach out to the rogue Imen. I get the feeling that what he can't exactly tell us, he can show us or get others to tell us—like he did with Mose, for example," Blaze said.

"Jax said we should gather the Lords and tell them about Darius. Watch their expressions carefully," Caia added. "And if we get so much as a whiff of something being wrong, we have to get out of here as fast as we can. Blaze can fly us out directly to the western plains, and Avril can track Harper from there, till we find them and, hopefully, the rogue Imen tribe."

"That sounds like a good plan," I agreed, crossing my arms over my chest.

"I find it hard to believe that the other Maras knew about Darius and his plan," Fiona muttered. "Their own people died in those explosions. If this was a conspiracy, I imagine that the explosions would've been much more reduced, focusing on Darius exclusively. I saw his daughter during the funeral service, and when we pulled out what was supposed to be her father's remains. That grief—"

"Seemed genuine, yes," Caia said. "I agree. But, nevertheless, we should do as Jax suggested. Round them up in one room and break the news. See how they react."

"And what about Zane?" Fiona asked, seemingly confused. "I mean, yeah, he did save me, and he did let me go, but he also abducted me in the first place. And if he's a prince, then... then he's high up on the food chain. He's got power and influence. He's the king's son! Why did he help you?"

"I'm not sure," Caia sighed. "From what he told us, it doesn't seem like he's got the greatest relationship with his father. Sure, he's a tad arrogant and probably spoiled, like all other royalty, but he did help us out of that meranium box. He guided us to our meeting spot, and he even showed us a way out of the palace. He could've told us that the statues turned into real creatures, but hey... I imagine this was his first act of rebellion."

"I don't think his brothers suspect him of aiding us," Blaze added.

"And that might work in our favor later," Fiona concluded with a nod.

"In the meantime, Harper and the others are out there with the rogue Imen," Caia said. "I think they have all, and I mean *all,* the answers we need."

"Well, I'm glad to see you two alive and well," Patrik replied, then looked at us. "Okay, time for a new action plan."

"Oh, goody, another one." Heron chuckled. "Maybe we'll get it right this time!"

"Avril, Heron, you two check in with the fallen Imen." Patrik nodded. "They're somewhere on the other side of the infirmary. See if they can tell you anything about the illness. See how they're doing, and, if you see anything stranger than... usual, I guess, let us know. You'll have to be stealthy and sneak in, though. We don't want anyone knowing you're talking to them. This whole slumber before death business is seriously starting to reek of foul play, and, until we get some answers, we can't even bring the issue up with the Lords. We still have to use diplomacy at this point."

"Duly noted," I replied. Heron straightened his back and came to my side.

"Fiona, Scarlett, Blaze, and Caia will stay here with me, while we summon the Lords and tell them what we've discovered so far in the daemon city, including what Darius has done," Patrik continued. "But before we split up, I need you all here with me for the spell I'm about to attempt on the asteroid belt. I need your energy."

"Ah, yes, the Druid dark arts," Heron quipped. "Count us in."

The night had settled over the mountain when we went outside on the terrace. Several Correction Officers stood guard on the edge, but none said anything. They didn't even look at us, and we didn't mind it, either. Cadmus's words from earlier were still ringing in my head. We couldn't really trust anyone.

Patrik and Scarlett set up the disruption spell, drawing a large chalk circle, with a triangle within it and a multitude of symbols along the edges. They placed various herbs and crystals at the triangle corners, and then Patrik handed us small, clear crystals to hold.

"Hang on to these," he said. "They'll help me draw the energy I need for this."

We all gathered around him, and he muttered a spell under his breath, lifting one hand in the air, clutching a larger, similar crystal, as he looked up at the sky.

I glanced down and noticed my clear pebble light up a warm, incandescent yellow. The others glowed the same, as delicate tendrils of what seemed like energy flowed out of them and into the crystal in Patrik's hand.

A few seconds passed. His stone brightened up with the intensity of a small star, forcing us to narrow our eyes so it wouldn't blind us. He uttered the last part of his chant, and a thick beam of light shot from his crystal straight into the sky,

headed straight for the seemingly endless string of glimmering purple asteroids in the sky.

It hit what looked like an invisible shield high up in the
atmosphere. It burst and dissipated into a rain of amber
sparks, but it never reached the asteroid belt. The spell didn't
work. My shoulders dropped, a familiar ache taking hold of
my stomach.

"Damn it," Patrik cursed, looking at his hand. The crystal
was clear and dull once more.

"It didn't work," Scarlett murmured, her voice barely
audible.

"It's not the asteroid belt," he replied, then stared at us with
what seemed like a mixture of anger and disbelief.

"Wait, what do you mean?" I blinked several times, as if
pulled back from a daze.

"It's this damn planet!" he said, gritting his teeth. "There's a
shield up there. The same thing that almost killed you the
other night, Avril. It's... It's a spell. It's swamp witch magic."

"Whoa..." Heron breathed. "How do you know *that*?"

"I don't have my notes from the swamp witches' tome with
me, but I remember reading about it. Viola was halfway
through with translating it. It was one of the most powerful
spells that the swamp witches had ever devised," Patrik
replied. "I took some notes from her at the time, and I was
waiting for her to finish. This was shortly before Jovi and
Anjani's wedding. The day before, to be precise. I'm certain.
This is incredibly powerful swamp witch magic. Nothing an

amateur could easily pull off, either. This is the heavyweight stuff."

We stared at each other for a while as we came to terms with the discovery. My breath hitched as I understood the full meaning of this.

"We are in so much trouble." I whispered my conclusion.

"Why do you say that?" Heron frowned at me.

"She's right," Patrik sighed, his hands resting on his hips. "This is a powerful obstruction. No Telluris, no interplanetary travel, nothing that could penetrate Neraka's atmosphere. And given that Rewa was able to get out and we were able to get through last week, it's recent. We need to find out who cast the spell, and break it at the source."

"The source..." I murmured. "Who could it be? They might still be alive, right? Since it's recent?"

"I believe so, yes." Patrik nodded. "This must be what's stopping GASP from getting to us, too. It's probably why we haven't seen any of our people coming in yet. This is a *huge* spell to perform, though."

"And the Maras are swearing up and down that they don't have that much knowledge," Fiona chimed in. "On the other hand, we've seen the daemons. They're way savvier with this stuff."

"I concur," Caia said. "The charmed collars, the invisibility spell... the cloaking charm on their tunnel entrances... I think they might be the real culprits here."

"And Darius? Maybe he's involved, too, since he's all

buddy-buddy with them now?" I replied, a wave of red-hot anger bursting through me. My hands balled into fists. Boy, was I going to break his face...

"One thing is certain," Patrik said. "The Lords need to know about this, too. Someone is actively trying to keep us here, on Neraka."

"Somebody doesn't want us to leave," I added.

I looked out into the night, at the gorges rising heavily a couple of miles away, on the other side of the plains. There was nothing but darkness—no movement, no glimmering red eyes, just the rustling of leaves around us as the winds grew stronger.

We were stuck here. And we'd become the targets of a surprisingly well-designed plot that aimed to get us all in meranium boxes. One question remained: who was behind it?

## 28

# HARPER

## (DAUGHTER OF HAZEL & TEJUS)

As soon as we reached the rogue Imen's settlement, Caspian was taken to the side and placed inside a sturdy iron cage, while Vesta motioned for us to move forward. A large tent awaited ahead, beyond the campfire.

"Is that really necessary?" I raised an eyebrow at her, and she responded with a shrug.

"Like I said, be thankful we're not killing him," she replied. "It's not often we get a Mara Lord walking into our village. We have younglings and defenseless elders to protect."

I scoffed and followed her as she led us deeper into the settlement, with Hansa and Jax right behind me. We were greeted with wary murmurs and wide, curious eyes. Children hid behind their mothers, and young male Imen stepped forward, holding their spears in sight. Their message was clear, imprinted on their faces. One wrong move and that was it.

It was neither my place nor my inclination to explain how quickly just Jax and I, fully grown adult vampires, could kill them, if given no other choice. We were here to get answers, not to measure our battle prowess.

We were taken into the large tent, where three Imen stood. They were in their mid-fifties, with long, dark hair braided with orange thread. Dark green cloaks covered their bodies, and a multitude of painted wooden medallions hung from around their slender necks. The one in the middle was a male, with a stern look in his brown eyes, while the other two were females, and just as unyielding and concerned about our presence here. They gave Vesta a questioning glance.

"These are the outsiders who helped us get our people back the other day," she explained briefly. "The Mara who was with them is in a cage outside. They claim him as their friend."

"Why is he still breathing, Vesta?" the male asked.

"Because he is here to help us," I replied, keeping my chin up. "He's risked his life for us to get here. His loyalty is indisputable to us, and he will not hurt anyone here."

"Speak for yourself, little girl," the female on his left shot back. "We've known his kind for millennia. They are anything but harmless."

"I'm trying to be respectful," I said, my teeth gritting and my anger bubbling just beneath the surface. "I would appreciate the same in return."

"I think we're getting off on the wrong foot here." Hansa stepped forward, accompanied by Jax. The three Imen immediately glowered at him, then at Vesta.

"He's one of them! Why isn't he in a cage, Vesta?" the male growled.

"He's not from Azure Heights. He's an outsider," Vesta replied with a frown. "He saved me and my people! And so did Lord Kifo. The only reason he's in a cage is because I don't want the three of you going mental on me before you even listen to what these people have to say."

Several seconds went by as our groups measured one another from head to toe, making mental assessments. I tried to figure out the best way to proceed with what was already a fragile conversation. I took a deep breath, then offered a polite nod.

"I'm Harper Hellswan, a vampire. This is Hansa Gorria, a succubus, and Jaxxon Dorchadas, a Mara, both of Calliope. They belong to the world which expunged the Maras of Azure Heights thousands of years ago," I said, trying to keep things as brief as possible. We needed to get answers, fast.

"Calliope belongs to Eritopia, a galaxy very far away," Jax added. "Harper here is from another world altogether. Her people established GASP, a group dedicated to protecting the innocents throughout this vast universe, including yourselves. We've aligned ourselves with them, as we wish to bring peace and balance to the many worlds around us. Yours is one of them."

"You mean to tell us that the Maras are a peaceful people, where you come from?" the female on the right asked, genuinely surprised.

"Yes," he replied. "We had our dark days, but they came to an end when we exiled those of us who wanted to kill others for blood. That happened thousands of years ago, and we never heard from them again until last week, when they reached out to us for help. We are here to investigate the disappearances that have plagued Azure Heights, but what we've uncovered so far is much worse than what we thought."

"They think the Maras are the victims here." Vesta raised an amused eyebrow at us, and suddenly I felt like the biggest stooge in the tent, for no apparent reason. What was she implying, exactly?

"You don't even know the half of it, then," the male Iman said, then gave us a curt bow. "I am Amund, and these are Eristhena and Ledda. We lead this tribe of Free People. Welcome to our humble Ambra. Or what is left of it, anyway."

"Ambra?" I asked.

"It was once a glorious, beautiful city about fifty miles from here to the west. Only ruins stand in its place today," Amund replied.

"What happened to it? And why don't you think the Maras of Azure Heights are victims? Their people have been taken by daemons, just like yours," Hansa interjected.

Amund wore a bitter smile as he motioned for us to sit down on a bunch of cushions that Vesta placed on the floor.

We settled onto them, and they took their seats in front of us. Vesta came next to me, sitting so she could see all of us at once.

"I'm afraid the people of Azure Heights have deceived you," Amund said, while Eristhena and Ledda nodded slowly, their gazes fixed on Jax. I figured they were having a hard time picturing him as our friend, judging by the still-surprised looks on their faces. "You see, we have been fighting both daemons and Maras for millennia. Our people are a commodity for both species. We are food."

My stomach dropped as the horrible truth sank in. Even without any further details, certain snippets of what we'd seen so far started to fall into place. And the picture I was getting turned my blood into ice.

"It wasn't always like that," Amund continued. "The daemons used to eat raw flesh, hunting animals and leaving us alone. One of their witch doctors, a crazy old fool by the name of Tural, discovered a way to consume souls, so he could keep himself younger. They already lived long lives. Some even made it to five thousand years before giving their last breath, and yet... it wasn't enough. At first, the daemons were shocked and rejected Tural, but he managed to persuade the others to do the same. Mind you, this was before the Maras arrived. They started hunting us for our souls, and our world started to decay, slowly but surely."

"They were stronger, faster, and downright vicious," Eris- thena added. "We didn't stand a chance, at first. As Imen, we built beautiful things, we worshipped nature, and we said grace for another day spent in this beautiful world. We didn't care for wars and violence. The daemons, on the other hand, seemed born for it."

"Then the Maras came," Ledda said, "in a ball of light. At first, we thought they were our saviors. We looked to them for help. And, in return, they killed us off, one by one, so they could drink our blood. It just went from bad to worse for the Imen. The Maras settled on the mountain and forced our people to build their city for them. Thousands died so Azure Heights could rise."

"In the end, we were forced to fight off attacks from both the daemons and the Maras. Our allies perished over the centuries. The Tolmacs, the Forest Spirits, the Daeris... As mighty and as wonderful as they were, the Maras' mind-bending and the daemons' claws got them in the end. Only we, the Free People, remained. Soon enough, both the Maras and the daemons were competing over us, while our numbers continued to drop."

"Wasn't there a truce between the Imen and the daemons?" I asked, remembering the totem in Shaytan's palace.

"For six full moons, yes," Amund replied. "But their addiction to souls was too strong. Then, shortly afterward, the Maras came. It was open season, really. We've been stuck between bloodsuckers and soul-eaters for thousands of years. They started capturing our people, forcing them into gated camps, forcing them to breed so they could have a steady supply of blood and souls. It went on like that for a long time, a wretched alliance of daemons and Maras. Until a couple of years ago, when they realized that their hunger was too strong for our species. We went from millions to a few thousand left standing today."

"By the Daughters..." Hansa gasped, her lower lip trembling, her eyes wide with horror.

"About three hundred years ago, the Maras learned a new trick from the daemons," Eristhena continued. "They consumed their first souls, and... they were hooked."

"Why? We're immortal." Jax frowned. "There is nothing for us to prolong by eating souls."

"It's the high," Amund replied. "The soul is a delicacy. It's pure energy flowing through one's veins. It gives them strength and vitality, and a feeling that everything is good and wonderful in the world. They became addicted to the alternate realities that they see when they consume souls... It's heartbreaking, really. We've watched so many of our own reduced to leathery corpses because the Maras wanted to 'get a taste of the heavens', as they called it."

"What about the Imen held captive?" I asked, my voice weak, my spine stiff.

"Imen bred in captivity didn't live for too long," Ledda explained. "They mostly died young, followed by mass suicides. There was no point to living, was there? All they ever saw was a patch of sky and the fangs of Maras and daemons. Their horrible attempt to treat us like cattle didn't last forever. Their food sources have been dying out."

"What about the Imen living in Azure Heights?" Jax replied.

"Their brains are wiped." Amund sighed. "They've been mind-bent out of... well, out of their minds. They're puppets, with clear sets of commands. They live under the illusion of a normal life, but, as soon as the clock strikes midnight, the Maras start to feed on them—mostly for blood. The ones they imprison are used exclusively for their souls. But the ones in the city are thoughtless and submissive, and they all die young. Few get to be in their forties. You see, repeated exsanguination leads to a disease they refer to as—"

"The slumber before death," I croaked, finally seeing everything clearly for the first time. My heart thudded as I thought of my friends back in Azure Heights, not knowing what fresh hell they'd been left in. And then my mind wandered over to Caspian. He knew. And I couldn't even process that yet.

"Exactly." Amund nodded. "Gradual consumption of blood weakens us, and our hearts eventually give up."

Hansa, Jax, and I stared at each other. It all made sense in the most heartbreaking way. And, judging by Jax's livid expression, he was taking it the hardest. It was no wonder, since his people had exiled these Maras to show mercy.

"We sent them away because they swore they would do better," he muttered. "If my grandfather... If we'd known what they would do to your people... I swear, Amund, we would've killed them all, right then and there. I am so sorry."

"I doubt your people knew exactly how vicious these Maras were. They put on a good show, don't they?" Amund scoffed, shaking his head.

"Wait, what about us? Why are we here, then?" I asked, suddenly alarmed beyond any form of self-control. "They came to us, asking for help. Their people vanishing... Was that a hoax, too?"

"More or less," Amund replied. "They tend to make those who disagree with them disappear, if they cannot control them. And I'm not talking about the Imen anymore. Perhaps this will ease your Mara friend's mind. Not all Maras are evil. Some really wanted to just live off the blood of the animals. Those who object to Azure Heights's practices, however, tend to... disappear. They're usually stuffed in that wretched prison of theirs or, worse, handed over to the daemons. A Mara's soul tastes particularly good, we hear."

"Oh, wow," I managed, rubbing my face with my palms, as if hoping it would wake me from what seemed like a nightmare.

"We are dying out," Ledda said. "The Maras and the daemons are conspiring to bring other species to Neraka. They started with you, a small group, to test their alliance and see what the best way would be for them to bring over a few dozen Eritopians and force them to breed in captivity."

"Like they did with the Imen," Hansa murmured.

"Exactly," Vesta replied. "They're hoping that other species, such as the Eritopian Maras, the Tritones, the Bajangs...

whoever they can get their hands on, really, can withstand life in a cage better than the Imen."

"How do you know about the Tritones and the other species from Eritopia? What have you heard? Where did you hear it from?" I bombarded her with questions.

"We have ears all over. We hear them, sometimes, when they're out hunting in the gorges, when they think no one is listening." Vesta smirked. "You thought the daemons owned the Valley of Screams? A handful of our own have learned to move through the ravines completely undetected. They're not invincible, you know."

"By the Daughters," Hansa blurted. "The Druid delegation, the swamp witch magic!"

"Ah, yes." Amund nodded. "The worst thing to ever happen to this planet. They crash-landed here thousands of years ago. They hoped the Maras would help heal their swamp witch, so they could be on their way... Poor souls. They never made it out. We don't know for certain what happened to them, but we are certain that the swamp witch is still alive, somewhere on this planet. Maybe in one of the daemon cities."

"We don't know what happened to the others, but we've assumed it's where I hail from." Vesta shrugged. "Like I said, I don't remember anything from the moment Amund and the others found me, facedown in the river, but we think my parents were part of that delegation, and that they somehow escaped, had me, and... I don't know..."

"You mean to tell me the swamp witch is still alive?" Hansa

replied, her eyes nearly popping out, before she looked at Jax. "Do you know what that means?"

"First of all, it means they've been somehow holding her hostage for her magic," Jax muttered, piecing everything together, while the Imen nodded. "And she hasn't been giving them everything at once, otherwise they would've already killed her. We didn't know much about the swamp witches' magic, about how it actually worked, back when we exiled these bastards. Chances are they don't know that they could perform all the swamp witch magic without... well, without the swamp witch."

"It means she was smart. She *is* smart, and keeping herself alive. And she's the very last of her kind, too," Hansa added.

"Then all these disruptions... Telluris not working, the interplanetary spell, the invisibility spell, the charmed collars... It's all because of swamp witch magic, isn't it?" I concluded, my stomach sinking lower.

"Let me guess, they blamed the asteroid belt?" Vesta replied, the corner of her mouth twitching.

"You know about that?" I murmured.

"Of course," she scoffed. "It's just the stuff of legend... mostly. Sure, the asteroids do help with concealing our planet —we know that much from the Imen's history—but it does nothing to prevent whatever spells you've attempted so far. That's all swamp witch magic disrupting you. They don't want you reaching out to anyone for help. They want to be in full control. And yes, they want you in cages, most likely making babies, so they can replenish their food source."

"That sounds… ugh, just sick." I fought to hold back the bile from coming up through my throat, as I could finally see Azure Heights for what it was. A most terrifying place, a nightmare with beautiful façades and bloodthirsty creatures who'd learned nothing from their erroneous ways.

"There is another daemon city a couple hundred miles to the north from here," Amund said. "Rumor has it that it's where the rest of the Druid delegation is kept. The few who've survived since they were detained here, anyway. We're thinking it might be where they're keeping the swamp witch, too, but we have no way of knowing that for sure. It is too risky for us to try to get in there."

I shot to my feet, rage coursing through my veins in waves of hot and cold, my heart aching as I walked out of the tent. I needed to see Caspian. And—

"Harper, wait!" I heard Hansa, as she got up and followed me, along with Jax, Vesta, and the three Imen.

Caspian heard me approaching and stood up, his hands still bound and his eyes covered. He listened quietly as we stopped in front of his cage. My heart was pounding, and he'd probably noticed that already.

"You knew," I hissed. "You knew! About everything! You knew!"

He didn't reply. Instead, he lowered his head.

"Lord Kifo is one of the leaders of Azure Heights," Amund

replied dryly. "Of course he knew. My only question is why he's here, with you."

"Caspian!" I raised my trembling voice. "Say something!"

I only got silence in return. It angered me beyond the point where I could be reasoned with. I lashed out and smacked the iron bars, bending them inward. Hansa pulled me back, and Caspian turned his head, his lips tightened into a thin, small line.

"You knew! You bastard! Is that why you've been telling us to go away? Is that the oath that kept you from telling us the truth? Is your word more important than the millions that your people have killed for their blood and their freaking souls? Huh? Talk to me! Tell me the truth!"

"He can't." Vesta's voice came into focus, and we all looked at her.

She narrowed her eyes at him, then moved closer to the cage.

"He can't? Is that really a good excuse at this point in time?" I spat, the pain in my chest blaring and bringing tears to my eyes. I felt betrayed. I'd fallen for him, and... he'd known about all this. My mind wasn't equipped to deal with this kind of disappointment. My body wasn't cut out for this type of emotional pain. It rippled through me, pinching at every nerve ending until my knees softened, and I leaned against Hansa for support.

"No, I mean he *can't*. He literally can't," Vesta replied, then pointed at his head. "Lord Kifo, please turn your head to the left and take a couple of steps forward. They need to see it."

"What are you talking about?" Jax frowned, then stilled as Caspian moved, showing the back of his right ear. "Oh..."

"What?" I breathed, craning my neck so I could see.

There was a small symbol tattooed there, in black ink. It was different from the red mark seared into the left side of his neck—that symbolized his status as an Exiled Mara, and all the Maras in Azure Heights had it. But the black mark was different, several geometric shapes fused into one.

"What is that?" Jax asked.

"I think it's a blood oath," Vesta replied. "I've seen it on a couple of Maras who fled from Azure Heights a few weeks back."

"Fled?" Hansa raised an eyebrow.

"Yeah, some manage to get out of there with their dignity and their bodies intact. But they're rare, believe me," Vesta explained briefly. "The mark is swamp witch magic, for sure. It's extremely powerful and deadly. No wonder he couldn't tell you anything: it would kill him before he even finished the first sentence. He has sworn not to tell specific things, and I imagine everything we've told you so far is part of those... specific things."

"So Lord Kifo hasn't been able to tell us the truth because of that mark?" Hansa concluded, frowning as she stared at Caspian.

"Exactly." Vesta nodded. "I think it all makes sense now,

even to me, as to why he's here with you all. He's been helping you, and he brought you here so you could learn the truth he couldn't tell you himself."

I needed a couple of minutes to gather my thoughts. My rage, fully justified until Vesta's revelation, was beginning to subside. Putting myself in Caspian's shoes for a second, I even understood why he'd done everything this way. All the warnings, they'd been genuine. He'd probably thought we'd be daemon chow and wanted us out of here before they sealed the planet off with swamp witch magic.

All the help he'd given us. The meranium pendants. His incursion into the daemon city with us. Our encounter with Mose. Even us coming here—these things had all been part of his elaborate plan to tell us the truth without uttering a single word himself. Like some sort of loophole for the blood oath. I covered my mouth with my hands as I realized exactly how true his words had been when he'd said that the lives of many depended on his oath. His was definitely one of them.

"You're protecting others, too, aren't you?" I breathed, inching closer to his cage. "Other Maras, Imen... When you said the lives of many depended on you... You're... You're really trying to help us, without getting yourself killed."

"I am sorry, Miss Hellswan," he replied, his voice faded and hoarse. "Perhaps this will help you understand the nature of my oath. Yes, I know everything. I know that Darius faked his death. He sacrificed some of our own people to make it look real, genuine..."

Blotches of red blossomed on his skin, smoke rising from beneath his collar. My throat closed up as I witnessed the effect of his blood oath.

"It was all meant to break your group apart, and get the dragon underground. As long as you have Blaze running loose, they're not going to accomplish much. They're terrified of him... Argh..."

He fell to his knees, third-degree burns eating away at his face.

"Stop! Stop it!" I cried out, gripping the iron bars. "I get it. It's true. The oath, I can see what it's doing to you!"

"I'm sorry, Harper," he groaned, breathing heavily as he regained his composure. His wounds were starting to heal already, thanks to his Mara immune system. "I wish I could've told you everything from the moment I first laid eyes on you."

"It's... It's okay, I get it," I replied softly. "I don't like it, obviously, but I get it. You did what you had to do."

"You know, I'm starting to think that Lord Kifo really isn't the bad guy we thought he was," Vesta mused, pursing her lips and crossing her arms over her chest. "They only do this to the Maras they can't fully trust, but don't want to kill yet. My guess is he pretended to go along with their plans, but, because he probably objected to their plans before, they forced him to take the blood oath and prove his allegiance. It's what I would do, anyway, if I were him."

"Something still doesn't make sense to me," Hansa replied, leaning against one of the iron bars as she turned to face us.

All around us, Imen moved, going about their business but giving us concerned glances. The guards stationed by Caspian's cage were quiet, but their eyes were fixed on us. I could only imagine what was going through their heads at this point.

One hell of a rescue team *we* were... Expertly duped by Exiled Maras.

"You said they plan to bring more Eritopians over here," Hansa continued. "How do they expect to achieve that? Granted, we cannot leave, nor contact our people. Our people can't get to us, either; otherwise you would've seen many more of us by now. How do they expect this to work?"

*Ah, yes, the million-dollar question.*

How were they going to get more of our own down here? Hansa was right, something really didn't click with the daemons' and Maras' plan. The logistics of accomplishing such a feat boggled my mind. No matter from which angles I tried to approach the problem, I couldn't see a solution.

Despite that massive unknown, I felt like I could finally breathe again. At least we had the truth. As terrible and as bloody as it was, we had it.

For the first time since we'd landed on Neraka, we *really* knew what we were dealing with. And we were horribly outnumbered and ill-equipped for it.

*But hey... at least we know what the heck is going on.*

# 29

## JAX

It was going to take some time to fully wrap my head around what we'd just learned. I struggled with my rage toward the Exiled Maras, and what they had done with their chance at a new, better life in this world. They'd gone from bad to worse. Not only were they still killing others for blood, they'd jumped to eating their souls, too.

They were beyond help. They had to be destroyed.

"We're not sure of the 'how' part yet," Vesta replied, referring to the Maras and the daemons' plan to get more Eritopians to Neraka. "But it must have something to do with whatever magic the swamp witch is giving them."

"They've gone to great lengths to get you here, in the first place," Amund said. "It's an elaborate play they've put together, with plenty of theatricals. They're using swamp witch magic and mind-bending to manipulate everything into this enormous dramatic performance. The Maras are playing the part of the victims, with the Imen by their sides as their faithful companions. Unfortunately for them, however, they have no control over the Free People."

"Their goal must be to capture and kill us, then reach out to Calliope again and ask for help," I concluded, my synapses firing. "But I still can't understand how they expect this to work. Chances are that GASP has already tried to reach out. Maybe they've been attempting to travel to Neraka, too. But since we haven't seen any of them, they clearly weren't able to get anywhere near the planet."

"I am sorry, we cannot answer these questions." Amund sighed. "But there is someone in the daemon city up north who might know more, since Lord Kifo here clearly can't shed any light without burning up."

"Our assumption is that the Maras didn't immediately try to capture you because they wanted to see how much you'd be able to figure out on your own, and how much they could get away with," Vesta mused. "My guess is that, once they saw the dragon, they realized they were in over their heads and couldn't immediately cage you because, well, dragon!"

"Oh, damn!" Harper gasped. "That makes so much sense! They were probably going to jump us the moment we landed on Neraka. Then they would've called for help. It's one thing to get an army of Maras and incubi, for example. The daemons and the Exiled Maras could handle them in large numbers, if GASP were to send in a battalion or something. But a dragon, no way. The moment they saw Blaze, the entire game changed. They probably didn't know we had dragons. In all fairness, Calliope didn't know we had dragons until Blaze and his father first came over for Jovi's wedding. It's hard to get them out of The Shade, in general."

"So they were probably going to act like victims, pretend we went missing, too, then call for more boots on the ground, whom they would immediately capture upon landing." Hansa nodded.

"Yes, Amund, we will definitely need to speak to whoever you have in that daemon city," I replied. "We need answers for these questions so we can understand exactly how they're planning to draw GASP in."

"The success of this performance will most likely dictate their next steps," Hansa added, looking at Caspian. "If they were able to fool us, they could very well be able to fool others. But as long as we're alive and free, they're in a pinch."

My terrified gaze met Harper's, as we both seemed to deal with the same bloodcurdling conclusion.

"The others are in danger," I muttered, staring at her.

"The Exiled Maras will know they screwed the pooch the moment they see Blaze and Caia," Harper breathed, and then her brow furrowed as something else dawned on her. "Hold on, they took Blaze down with that yellow powder back in daemon city. If he's really the one the Maras were afraid of, and given their alliance with the daemons, why didn't they use the yellow powder on Blaze when we were still in Azure Heights?"

Vesta and the other Imen thought about it for a couple of seconds. The fae's face lit up as she found the answer. "The powders are new," she said. "A few days, at most, and it's probably the latest charm that the daemons were able to pull out of the swamp witch. Chances are the Maras have yet to get their filthy claws on the stuff. And, frankly, I don't see the daemons giving it away so quickly. You see, they may be allies, but they certainly don't trust each other. I'm guessing that the daemons wouldn't give anything to the Maras that they could later use against them."

"How certain are you that the daemons won't pass it along to the Maras nonetheless?" I asked.

"It's just a speculation at this point. The one thing I know for sure is that all the stunning powders they're using are brand new. It's something we'll have to study and be prepared for. I'm not sure masks will prevent them from affecting us, if that stuff gets thrown into our faces."

A knot formed in my throat. I knew the team stood a better chance with Blaze there, but I also knew that they had been able to capture him once with yellow dust. Nothing would stop them from trying again, if the daemons decided to share their powder secrets with the Maras.

# 30

## HARPER

### (DAUGHTER OF HAZEL & TEJUS)

"Okay, what next?" I asked, looking at Hansa and Jax. My friends were out there in Azure Heights, surrounded by monsters. "We need to tell Caia and the others. Like, now."

"I think you should stay here, and not risk capture," Vesta said. "I will send two of my best scouts to Azure Heights. They know every secret passage, every trail in the woods, every single access point into the city. Where will your friends be?"

"In the infirmary, most likely, on the second level," I replied.

"I'll have them go there right now, to warn your friends and get them out of the city." Vesta nodded, then snapped her fingers at two young Imen boys who had settled by the campfire. Their heads turned, their eyes wide as they stood and joined us. They couldn't be older than sixteen, but seemed spry and quick enough to do the job.

"Are you sure? Maybe one of us should go with them." Jax frowned.

"No need." Vesta gave him a confident wink. "My boys are fast and light on their feet. The Maras won't even know they're there. This isn't even their first time in Azure Heights. Besides, we only just got you here; I can't risk you getting captured while trying to get your friends out, when you don't even know that mountain as well as these two."

She put her hands on the boys' shoulders, and spoke in a somber, bossy voice.

"You two go to Azure Heights. You've seen the dragon, right?" she asked them, and they nodded. "Get him and his friends out of the infirmary on the second level. Take the eastern route in, the one with the red walls. You'll have to push some stones out of the way, but it will take you straight to that level, just fifty yards from the place. Be quiet, be fast, be smart. We'll wait for you here."

The Imen boys didn't wait a second longer. They immediately packed some water in leathery flasks, and dried bread for the road. They geared up with knives and covered themselves with dark green cloaks, and ran off into the dark night settling over the woods.

My heart thumped, but Vesta was right. The team was relatively better off with Blaze, and they'd already been warned to be wary of the Exiled Maras. All we could do was keep our fingers crossed and hope for the best.

We'd just escaped one daemon city—there was no way we were going to let some ghoulish Maras capture us instead. I stole a glance at Caspian, then shifted my focus back to Vesta.

"Have you been to that daemon city up north before?" I asked.

"A couple of times," she replied with a brief nod. "We have friends there. It might come as a shock, but they're daemons. They're pacifists, to be precise. Not on the king's good side."

"Hah, I knew it," I muttered, mostly to myself. "We were wondering if we could consider them potential allies."

"They are, though they're not easy to come across. They keep a low profile," Ledda said. "They're the ones who taught us about the ashes."

"The ashes," I mumbled, then remembered Mose's nifty little trick. "That's right, to stop daemons from picking up your scent."

"This whole village is surrounded by twenty feet of ashes, sprinkled into the grass." Ledda smiled. "We're safe here, and we've gone to great lengths to conceal our presence. We have scouts keeping watch on a two-mile radius, and traps set throughout the woods. You can all stay here while we wait for your friends."

"What about the daemon city up north? When can we go there?" I replied.

"As soon as your dragon gets here," Vesta sighed. "If I am to leave my village, I want to make sure there's a dragon protecting my people. The last time I left, they wound up in cages, and you helped me save them. Granted, we've moved camp here now, and we've taken additional measures to keep daemons at bay, but, still, I'm not comfortable with leaving them just yet."

"I'm sorry, but I'm not feeling too comfortable with us just staying here, while the kids are back there, with those monsters!" Hansa snapped, chewing the inside of her cheek.

"Trust me, my boys will get the job done, and fast," Vesta tried to assure her. "They keep indigo horses on the edge of the forest, and know the best and fastest routes through the Valley of Screams. We've stocked up on tricks over the past few centuries. We can handle a simple extraction."

"Besides, I doubt the Maras will get too aggressive. They only have the Imen in the city to feed on; they won't risk any more of their lives with a dragon on the loose," Jax added.

"The Lords don't like loose ends, but they've already stumbled across an unexpected hurdle with Blaze," Vesta said. "If anything, all my boys need to do is find the dragon and warn him. He'll get everyone on his back and fly out."

A minute passed as Hansa tried to accept the idea that she wasn't out there with the scouts. I understood her frustration well enough, but even she had to admit that we were better off here, hashing out the next stages of our plan.

"We can focus on finding the swamp witch and ending everything," I offered. "Once we get her to help us disrupt whatever spells these bastards are using, we can reach out to Calliope and bring in all our dragons."

"You're right." She exhaled sharply, then gave me a weak smile.

I looked at Caspian again, and noticed his satisfied expression, a faint smirk stretching his lips. His burns were almost fully healed, and my heart started to break a little, as I tried to imagine how tormented he must've been about all of this.

He'd been playing a dual role, trying to keep the Lords from suspecting him of treason, while helping us stay free and alive. He was one of the good guys, and the relief I felt upon thinking that took me by surprise. I wasn't just pleased that he wasn't a traitor; I was happy that I hadn't fallen for an evil creature.

"Will you let him out?" I looked at Amund. "He's already proven himself to you, to us."

"We're not comfortable with doing that just yet." Amund shook his head slowly.

"Why the hell not? He's just bound by a blood oath! He won't hurt anyone!"

"We will discuss it among ourselves soon, and we will decide in the morning." Amund raised his voice enough to remind me that he and his female companions were still in charge. "Vesta will see to your dinner and accommodation, and Lord Kifo will stay here, for the time being."

"Can you at least untie him? Take the blindfold off?" I wasn't ready to give up just yet.

"What if he tries to mind-bend the guards?" Ledda frowned.

"He won't," I said. "I'll stand guard. Jax will take turns with me, if needed."

"Agreed." Jax nodded firmly. "Please. I'm sure Lord Kifo won't put his life at risk like this. He knows how fast I can separate his head from his body. And so can Harper."

The Imen glanced at each other for a brief moment. Amund then looked at one of the guards. "Remove his restraints."

The guard came closer to the cage and asked Caspian to turn around and take a couple of steps back. Once he was within reach, the guard untied his hands and removed his blindfold. As soon as he could see again, Caspian looked at me, his jade eyes soft and... sad.

"Thank you," he murmured, rubbing his wrists.

"Just don't do anything stupid," Amund shot back, then motioned for Eristhena and Ledda to follow him back into the main tent, while we were left there with Vesta and two guards by Caspian's cage.

The scouts were out there, on their way to the city. My stomach churned, as I kept thinking about Caia and the others, trying to do some good for creatures who only deserved to get their heads chopped off.

With each minute that went by, my objective became clearer. I had to find the swamp witch. All our troubles would end once we got hold of her—the last of her kind, and the key to not only our freedom, but also to ending this war and saving whatever was left of the Imen species.

I had a bone to pick with both the daemons and the Maras, and I knew my turn would come to cut them down, one by one, and deprive them of the privilege of living.

My palms were starting to itch, the rage dull and permanent in the pit of my stomach.

*Stay there. I'll need you for later.*

# 31

## AVRIL

(DAUGHTER OF LUCAS & MARION)

There were two other doors at the back of the infirmary, leading into the other care rooms. Heron and I snuck around the corner, taking advantage of the dark as we waited for the nurses to leave the one room that had its lights on. I'd caught the scent of Imen in there.

"I can hear their hearts beating," Heron whispered, his face dangerously close to mine.

I took a deep breath, trying my best not to look at him. I could feel the tension between us, and I yearned to just wrap my arms around him whenever he got near me. My gaze was fixed on the one door we needed to see open.

"The Imen, you mean," I breathed.

"Mm-hm." He inched closer, making my spine tingle as his breath tickled my ear.

"Have you ever heard of personal space?" I muttered, mostly angry at my inability to control my reactions with him.

"What's that?"

I wasn't sure whether he was serious or joking, as his tone was flat, and I *really* didn't want to turn my head to look at him, afraid I'd lose my thoughts in those big jade eyes of his.

"It's an invisible area around a person, and it's best not to invade it without a good reason," I whispered, hoping I'd managed to at least conceal my frustration.

"And?"

*He's toying with me.*

"And you're in it. In mine, I mean," I replied.

"Does it bother you?"

"Are you freaki—" My head turned without me even realizing it, and I instantly regretted it, as I was met with a pair of green eyes that seemed to look right into my soul. My breath hitched, and I swallowed my words. We stood like that for a while, until his gaze dropped to my lips and heat expanded through my body, like I'd suddenly turned into an active volcano and was about to erupt.

A door creaked open, and we both looked back at the infirmary. I breathed a sigh of relief, knowing I'd been seconds away from doing the unthinkable and pressing my lips against his. Fortunately—or not—two Mara nurses came out, then went around the building, probably headed toward the stairs leading up to the next level.

"Coast is clear," I murmured, and left our hiding place.

I moved along the wall, then turned the knob and opened the door. We slipped inside, where two Imen lay in their beds. They were both males, in their late thirties. Their faces were pale, their eyes sunken, and their lips almost purple. According to Heron, they were still alive, but they didn't really look it.

"These two look like hell," Heron muttered as he moved closer to one of them, scanning him from head to toe.

"The slumber before death, I guess." I shrugged, and moved around the beds to check on the other Iman, the one we'd seen collapse earlier outside Marion's perfume shop. I nudged him gently, and he moaned in response, but didn't wake up.

I glanced up to see Heron shaking the other Iman in his bed.

"What in the world?" I exclaimed, scowling at Heron, who gave me a most innocent look.

"What?" he asked.

"He's not a ragdoll! You can't just shake him like that!" I couldn't believe I had to explain that, my hands resting on my hips.

"He's not responsive."

"Clearly, otherwise he would've slapped you by now," I muttered, then froze, my eyes wide open. A relatively familiar scent was in the vicinity, and getting closer. "Crap, the nurses!"

I looked around and noticed a wooden screen in the corner of the room. Grabbing Heron's arm, I rushed behind it, and held my breath as the door opened. In walked one of the nurses who had treated Patrik. I could see her face through one of the tiny holes on the edge of the screen. No wonder the scent was familiar—it was a mixture of wildflowers and honey, and it was definitely *her* fragrance. My nose never lied.

We watched quietly as she walked over to the first Iman's bed, briefly glancing over her shoulder at the closed door. She pursed her lips, raised a dissatisfied eyebrow, then looked at the unconscious Iman.

She bent over, bringing her face close to his neck. My heart stopped when she removed a scalpel from a nearby drawer and made a small incision behind the Iman's ear, muttering something under her breath.

"I can't believe I'm reduced to leftovers from the rich bastards upstairs," she grumbled, then parted her lips. Little wisps of white light came out from the Iman's open wound and slipped into her mouth.

Caia and Fiona had described the eating of souls to us before.

*Oh my*. The nurse was eating an Iman's soul. The Mara was consuming a soul. *What the—*

I didn't even realize I had gasped until I heard myself, and instantly covered my mouth. Heron's eyes were wide with shock. The nurse's back snapped straight, and she looked directly at the wooden screen in front of us.

I heard Heron sigh. Crap. She knew we were here.

There was no point in hiding. She'd probably noticed our

heartbeats by now, already alarmed enough by the gasp to pay attention.

Heron was the first to step away from the screen, and I followed, glowering at her. She sneered, baring her fangs at us. It was enough to set me off.

"Are you serious?" I snapped.

She came at us fast, but she didn't stand a chance. I dodged her elongated claws, and Heron whipped his sword out and beheaded her before she could even turn around. Her head rolled on the floor, blood pooling at our feet.

"She ate his damn soul." I cursed under my breath, then rushed over to the Iman to check for his pulse. Nothing. I glanced up at Heron and swallowed back tears. It broke my heart to see what was happening to the Imen, as it all came into focus. "He's dead."

Heron's shoulders dropped, blood still dripping from his sword. "We need to go tell the others. *Now.*"

"Heron. They are eating souls." I had to say it out loud, somehow having trouble processing the information. It didn't make sense. Why? How? For how long had the Maras been doing this? So many questions flooded my head, I found it difficult to breathe and focus. "The Maras... are eating *souls.*"

"Yeah, I can *see* that," he replied bluntly, much better at keeping his cool than I was.

"Don't tell me you saw this coming!"

He thought about it for a couple of seconds, then

shrugged. "The thought did cross my mind, but it sounded too absurd to even be considered as a potential reality."

"Well then, what do you think of this?" I replied, my voice dripping with sarcasm.

"Avril, we need to go." Heron tried to keep me on track.

The door opened again, and we both froze as six more nurses came in. They all came to a halt when they saw us, the bloody sword in Heron's hand, and the decapitated Mara by the wooden screen. Their synapses seemed to function well, as they instantly hissed, baring their fangs at us.

"Seriously?" I groaned, incredibly annoyed as I drew my sword, anger pouring through my veins like liquid fire.

One of them shut the door. "Like that'll stop us from getting out of here," Heron scoffed, glowering at the six Maras.

"You're ruining dinner." One of them grinned.

My hand gripped the sword to the point where my knuckles turned white. Not one of them was walking out of here alive. I was going to make sure of that. One by one, their heads would fall.

And afterward, I'd get some time to properly experience the shock I'd just had to set aside.

I shot Heron a brief glance, and he gave me a nod in return.

"Sorry, but you're going on a diet as of tonight, ladies," I replied.

I dashed forward and left no room for debate.

## 32

## FIONA

### (DAUGHTER OF BENEDICT & YELENA)

Patrik, Scarlett, Blaze, Caia, and I waited outside the infirmary for the Lords to come down for their briefing. Avril and Heron were on the other side, looking in on the sick Imen who had collapsed during the day.

It was close to eight in the evening. The dark purple sky held its myriads of stars above us, and the first of three moons gave off a warm white glow. Flames flickered in the street-lamps lining the massive terrace overlooking the plains and the distant gorges—the latter still sending shivers down my spine whenever I settled my gaze on their black silhouettes.

Six Correction Officers waited by the main road that connected the first level and the plains to the rest of Azure Heights. They never made eye contact with us, and barely moved as we watched the Lords come down—Emilian, Rowan, Farrah, and Rewa, along with Vincent.

After our suspicions of their behavior toward the Imen had been reignited during the day, and after adding the possibility that they might've also known about Darius's betrayal, I had a hard time looking at Vincent with the same kindness I'd mustered before. Distrust ate away at me, and I couldn't shake the feeling that this conversation could go south, fast. I'd shared my angst with Patrik, and he'd told me to just stay focused and alert, and watch out for anything suspicious in their behavior.

*Like that'll be easy with these folks.*

"Good to see you're back." Emilian greeted us with a broad smile, looking at Blaze and Caia before he glanced behind us. "Where are Jax and the rest of your team?"

"They're out in the western plains," Caia replied with a polite nod, as the Lords gathered in front of us.

"Hello, Fiona." Vincent winked, and I felt my skin crawl. Whatever was nagging me, his open advances weren't doing anything to remove the tension from my body.

"What are you doing down here, Vincent?" I replied. "Not meaning to sound disrespectful, but I believe we sent word for just the Lords to attend this briefing."

It took him a couple of seconds to respond, his expression unwaveringly positive. "Mother wants me to be more active in these meetings. She's looking to retire."

I shifted my gaze to Rowan, who responded with a dry

smile. I'd struck a nerve, for sure. The air between us all was thickening with every minute that went by.

"What are they doing in the western plains?" Emilian didn't wish to gloss over Harper and the others' whereabouts.

"We did our survey of the daemon city, and decided it would be best if we covered more ground by splitting up," Caia said, her chin high. "They wanted to reach out to the rebel Imen, and we came back to update our team and your lordships."

"What could they possibly want from the rebel Imen?" Farrah scoffed, while Rewa kept her gaze fixed on Blaze— something that Caia totally noticed and did not like, judging by the muscle nervously twitching in her jaw. "They're food for those wretched daemons. They can barely defend themselves out there!"

"Jax thought it would be good to talk to them nonetheless," Caia replied. "They're much closer to the daemons than you are, geographically speaking. They could shed some light, provide some insights from their encounters with the creatures."

"I doubt that, but anyway, tell us about the daemon city." Farrah smirked.

"It's big," Caia shot back bluntly. "There are more of them than we'd initially thought. Their swamp witch magic is stronger and much more diverse, too. We saw their king."

The Lords stilled. I couldn't tell much from their expressions, though, other than the fact that they were stunned.

"The king of daemons?" Emilian frowned slightly. Caia nodded in response. "What did he seem like to you?"

I would've gone for 'What was he like?'. He probably meant exactly that, but the way he formulated his question left room for misunderstanding, and even doubt. There it was again, that claw in my stomach...

"Big. Menacing. Fearless and determined," Caia said. "Won't take no for an answer. Leads his people with an iron fist. Blaze and I were captured for several hours, until Jax, Harper, Hansa, and Caspian helped get us out."

She was careful to leave Zane's name out of it. *Good, we can't risk revealing potential allies and putting them at risk, after all.*

Their eyes were wide with surprise and concern, and Emilian took a step forward. "Are you all right? Did they hurt you?"

"No, they were going to eat our souls later," Blaze replied. "According to the king of daemons, we're quite the delicacy, compared to the Imen."

"I just... I don't understand. I still can't wrap my head around this whole soul-eating thing. It's so... ghastly. Why would they do it?" Rowan shook her head slowly, her mouth crooked with disgust.

"Sustenance. A single soul keeps them sated for days, brimming with strength and energy of unnatural levels. It prolongs their lives, too," Caia explained. "In the absence of souls, raw meat seems to do the trick, but, you know, they obviously prefer souls. Apparently, it's exhilarating to feel some-one's life force flowing through you."

Farrah, Rowan, and Rewa collectively covered their mouths to stifle their gasps and groans. I couldn't really blame them. The entire concept made my stomach turn inside out, too. My mind wandered back to Zane for a brief moment, wondering if he took the same pleasure in consuming souls. A shiver ran down my spine, and I looked up at Vincent. His gaze was fiercely attempting to pierce through my very soul, pushing me further to the edge.

"That's... That's horrific," Rewa mumbled, visibly distraught.

"So, Lord Kifo is with Miss Hellswan and the rest of your team, then?" Emilian changed the subject.

"Yes," came Caia's reply. "I haven't gotten to the juiciest part of our visit to the underground, though."

"Pray tell, what's that?" He raised an eyebrow.

"Well, I can tell you there is one Mara who knows the king of daemons very... very well."

The Lords frowned, then looked at each other before they stared at Caia, waiting for her to continue. But she wasn't done with stringing them along. She carefully observed their expressions, then gave Scarlett and me a brief sideways glance.

"Go on?" Rewa seemed impatient and somewhat irritated. My guess was that she was no longer bothering to hide her dislike of Caia, given their shared interest in Blaze. It really didn't take a scientist for either of us to know that our little fire fae and the dragon were getting closer each day, while Rewa's advances flew right past his ears. There was bound to be some friction, sooner or later.

"Your father," Caia said.

Several seconds passed as Rewa blinked with confusion.

"My father?"

"Darius, Lord of House Xunn, is besties with the king of daemons," Caia replied.

"That's... No, that's impossible! My father didn't even know about daemons until you brought their name up!" Rewa's anger translated into raw tremors in her voice, and her chest rose with each deep breath she took in an attempt to keep herself under control.

"Where did you hear that?" Emilian replied, his tone lower than usual, and his eyes narrowed. "The daemons told you? Who?"

"Darius himself." Blaze moved closer to Caia's side. "He's alive."

Rewa froze, her mouth gaping with shock.

"What are you talking about, Blaze? Have you lost your mind?" she murmured.

"Jax and Hansa saw him. He's alive. He faked his own death. The explosions were his doing." Caia reinforced Blaze's statement.

"No... That can't be. I buried my father! I saw his corpse... his Lordship ring..." Rewa shuddered, bursting into tears.

Vincent put his arm around her shoulders, pulling her closer as she sobbed uncontrollably.

Emilian, Farrah, and Rowan were quiet, occasionally stealing glances at one another.

"I'm sorry, Rewa, but it's true," Caia replied softly. "Darius is alive."

"It can't be!" she cried out. "My father wouldn't... he wouldn't do that to me. He wouldn't cause me so much grief."

The information didn't sit well with the Lords, a mixture of grief and anger settling on their faces. I caught movement out of the corner of my eye, and slowly turned my head to see Correction Officers lining the edge of the terrace on the third level, looking down at us. Why did that feel so wrong?

"I am truly sorry, Rewa," Blaze sighed. "He lied to you. He lied to all of us. We don't know why he did what he did. All we know is that he's alive and he is working with the daemons."

"You... You mean to tell us that Darius, a Lord of this city and a friend to us all, blew up our homes, killed our people, and aligned himself with Shaytan?" Emilian replied through gritted teeth.

My heart stopped for a second. My temperature dropped to icy new lows, as the hard truth hit me like a punch in the gut.

"Basically, yes, Lord Obara," Blaze replied. "The explosions were planned, devised to aid him in faking his death, but we—"

"You know his name," I breathed, every muscle in my body loaded with unbearable amounts of tension.

Emilian swiftly turned his head to look at me. "What are you talking about?"

"You said his name. Shaytan. You know the king's name," I said, my voice somewhat firmer as my brain adjusted to the revelation. I'd yet to figure out what it meant, exactly, but my mind was already in overdrive, and processing.

Patrik was the second to realize the gravity of what I'd just said. His forehead smoothed, his lips pressed tight as he glowered at Emilian, who in return gave us a very baffled expression.

"No, I didn't," he shot back.

"Yes, you did. You said 'Shaytan'," I insisted, suddenly feeling like I was being taken for an idiot.

"You told us his name." Emilian then flipped, changing his story. My hand slowly slipped down my side, looking for my sword handle.

"No, we didn't," Blaze replied. "We never mentioned his name."

The longest moment squeezed through in perfect silence as we all glared at the Lords, who seemed genuinely befuddled —except Emilian. He was getting angry. I could almost hear the blood bubbling in his veins. Nowhere as hot as mine in this instant, but still, he was raging on the inside.

He'd made a terrible mistake.

He'd given himself away. It suddenly became impossible to

think that the others didn't know about Darius. Emilian knew. Despite Caspian's oath of silence, it was safe to assume he was also aware. Would Farrah, Rowan, and Rewa be kept in the dark, then? Or Vincent, for that matter?

Rewa kind of answered that question when she burst into a short cackle, then wiped the crocodile tears from her face. My stomach dropped. It was one thing to suspect it, and a completely different thing to have your worst fears confirmed.

*The Lords were in on it... They're conspiring with the daemons!*

"You've got to be kidding me," Caia scoffed. "You all knew."

"In all fairness, they were bound to find out sooner or later." Vincent looked at his mother, who rolled her eyes, her displeasure obvious. They were all uncomfortably calm, considering what we'd just discovered about them. The knot in my stomach throbbed painfully, slowly making its way up into my ribcage.

"It didn't take them too long, though." Farrah nodded with what looked like some kind of sick, perverted appreciation toward us. *What the hell is going on here?*

"True. Had Emilian kept his stupid mouth shut, we could've stretched this for at least a couple more days, until we could catch Hellswan and her clique of self-righteous worms," Rowan spat. Emilian scowled at her.

"It was an innocent mistake!" he shot back.

My head turned from left to right between them, as if I had a front row seat at a tennis match. I really didn't know how to fully process this. They had simply transformed before our very eyes—from the graceful, eloquent, and innocent Maras to this bickering pack of monsters in expensive silks.

"Well, your 'innocent' mistake now makes you look like an idiot!" Rowan replied, raising an eyebrow.

"It takes one to know one," Emilian sneered.

"At least we don't have to pretend anymore." Rewa rolled her eyes.

"You people are sociopaths," Scarlett gasped. "Full-blown sociopaths. You've been acting this whole time. This... This was all just... theater..."

"Ah, she's catching on," Rewa snickered, crossing her arms over her chest. Her features had turned from soft and sweet, beneath that pixie haircut, to filthy and ice cold, as pure evil seemed to flicker in her jade eyes. "You're not as stupid as I thought. Consider it a compliment."

"Vincent," I muttered, noticing his cool demeanor, while Rowan, Farrah, and Emilian kept snapping at each other, hurling all kinds of insults. "You knew."

Our eyes met, but I could no longer recognize the Mara with reddish hair and pale green eyes. The Vincent I knew was gone. He was probably never real, anyway. The guy replacing him put on a mirthless smile, and I finally understood why my skin had been crawling whenever he'd looked at me. My instincts were never wrong. I'd gotten a whiff of what we were getting ourselves into from the moment Caia and Blaze had told us about Darius. Something just hadn't clicked for me then.

"My darling Fiona, of course I knew," Vincent replied. "We all knew. Did you really think Darius would do something without us signing off on it?"

In retrospect, he had a point. But the Maras and Imen who had died in the explosions had provided enough doubt for us to not immediately jump to that conclusion.

"You killed your own people with those explosions," I said, my fingers slowly curling over my sword handle. The cool ivory grip helped me focus on the next steps. We obviously had to do something, but I wasn't sure what.

"Collateral damage," Vincent replied. "We had to make it believable."

"And Lord Kifo?" Patrik asked, as I briefly caught a glimpse of the increasing number of Correction Officers gathering on our level as well. They were already surrounding us. "Was he a part of your plan? Was he in on it?"

Emilian, Farrah, and Rowan suddenly remembered that we were still there, partially crippled by sheer astonishment. "Oh, Lord Kifo knew," Rowan scoffed. "He couldn't do anything about it, though. He tried to be a rebel, but it didn't work out too well for him and his adoptive father. His parents tried the same crap, and look where that got them."

"So he was against all this," Patrik replied. I could see his gaze darting across the platform, as he registered the Correction Officers closing in a circle around us.

"Yes, that self-righteous little rat," Emilian muttered, hatred almost oozing out of him. "We tried to keep him in check. We even got him to swear a blood oath, just to make sure he wouldn't talk. I see he's decided to care more about some outsiders than his own people."

"If he was such a nuisance, why didn't you just kill him?" I asked.

"We tried to steer him back on the right track. He'd even promised that he was on our side, that he would never betray us. It's why we put him under that oath. We can't really kill off our own so liberally. It's not like there are so many of us, in comparison to daemons," Emilian said.

"What makes you think he won't tell Harper and the others the truth? How long do you think before he will break his oath?" I raised an eyebrow.

"It's not a regular oath he's under." Emilian grinned. "If he talks, he dies. We actually thought he was finally coming around. Then that harlot Hellswan showed up. That boy cannot see straight when she's around."

"You better mind your tongue," Caia hissed, flipping her lighters open.

Emilian and the others took a couple of steps back, visibly uncomfortable in the presence of raw firepower. Rewa snapped her fingers, and the Correction Officers moved closer toward us, their swords screeching as they left their scabbards.

It was about to get crazy, fast. I counted at least fifty of them on the second level with us, along with about thirty or forty on the third level above.

"What was your plan, exactly?" I growled, my gaze shifting

from Vincent to Emilian. "What were you hoping to get out of this, out of duping us?"

I needed to prolong this for as long as possible, to give myself and the others some time to think things through, and to come up with a smart exit plan. My only hope was that Avril and Heron were going to show up soon. We needed the extra pairs of hands.

"At first, we wanted to just capture you all as soon as you landed," Emilian said. "But then we saw the dragon, and, well, we didn't know how susceptible he was to our mind-bending. It was too soon for us to try anything, and, frankly, we wanted to see how well we could pull this off without throwing you all in cages. Know thy enemy and whatnot. We couldn't mind-bend any of you vampires and Maras, and we would've had to catch Blaze alone, without any of you to quickly figure it out. Much to my dismay, you kids just can't be apart for too long. Always together, always with your guard up. So, we decided it was best to simply let the daemons get you, sparing us the trouble of such an effort."

"Why, Lord Obara? Why are *we* here?" I asked, my muscles jerking with anticipation.

"Why, for sustenance," Rewa replied with a smirk. "Souls are incredible. The strength they give us, the energy they fill us with... You have no idea how wonderful that can be. Unfortunately, it is also addictive. Once we got into it, we didn't really want to stop. And why should we? We are so powerful and capable. Your presence here alone is a testament to that. Just look at how good our acting was, how convincing! The setting is perfect!"

"How is bringing us here an example of your intellectual prowess?" Caia retorted, no longer concerned about hurting anyone's feelings. I knew she'd held a lot back in previous days, when Rewa was giggling and flirting with Blaze. "We just discovered what you've been up to. And we have a dragon."

"And don't think I'll be holding anything back," Blaze added, straightening his back.

Rewa chuckled, then looked right into Blaze's eyes, hers shimmering gold. "Well, I don't know about that... Blaze, darling, do me a favor. Don't turn into a dragon. Don't use your fire against us."

*Oh, crap.*

Everything had happened so fast, the revelation so mind-boggling that none of us had thought to worry about the Maras' mind-bending ability affecting our non-vampire friends until this horrible reminder. If they'd been trying to earn our trust until now, by not attempting any mind-bending on our dragon, well... that was done. The cat was out of the bag. Blaze stilled, his expression blank and his arms limp. Caia gasped, then turned to face him, gripping his shoulders and desperately shaking him.

"Blaze! Don't listen to her! Blaze! Look at me! Please, look at me," she pleaded with him, but he was unresponsive. Rewa then giggled, making me really eager to chop her head off.

"Blaze, darling," she said. "Be a doll, choke the life out of

Caia. She was the first on my disposal list anyway. Not a soul I'm interested in tasting."

Before either of us could react, Blaze brought his hands up and grabbed Caia by the throat. Fires roared through me, and I drew my sword.

"You're not going to get away with this!" Patrik snarled, then tried to get between Blaze and Caia in an attempt to stop him from choking her.

"Of course we will!" Emilian laughed, his voice dripping with mockery and disdain. "We have something that you don't. We have a swamp witch."

All hell broke loose in the following second.

The Correction Officers came at us, their blades up. We immediately reacted, fighting back with everything we had. The Lords slowly shuffled toward the stairs, watching us with delight and amusement, as if we were putting on a great piece of entertainment for them.

Just as I'd originally thought, it got crazy fast. Scarlett flashed from one Mara to another, using her lightspeed to deliver swift and deadly blows. Her blade cut through Mara flesh with such ease, she could easily handle four to five opponents at once.

Patrik brought out both defensive and offensive Druid magic, blasting blue fireballs at the Correction Officers, alternating with heavy sword hits, while blocking attacks from the side. Had I not been so busy with my own share of enemies, I would've gladly sat back and watched him. The Druid had some insane fighting skills, as he'd already proven back in the gorges. I just couldn't get tired of it.

I unleashed my full strength on the Maras coming at me. Rage fueled me, and I spared no punches, striking viciously at my opponents. Blood gushed from their open throats, and I quickly moved to the next two Correction Officers who were bold enough to take me on. I heard bones cracking beneath my knuckles as I punched my way through the increasing crowd of hostiles.

I was trying to get to Blaze and Caia, as she was struggling to set herself free from his deadly grip. There was no way in hell that I was going to let any of my friends get hurt or die in this nicely decorated hellhole.

# 33

## CAIA

### (DAUGHTER OF GRACE & LAWRENCE)

Flashing little white stars were covering the image in front of me—an image I was having a hard time registering, despite the strong hands tightening against my throat and cutting off my air supply.

I knew Blaze didn't want to do this. Mind-bending was a powerful tool, especially in the hands of a giggling psychopath like Rewa. I caught a glimpse of her grinning with satisfaction as she watched from the edge of the stairs.

"Blaze... please, you're hurting me..." I croaked, unable to breathe.

My hands covered his, and I used all my strength in a desperate attempt to pry them from my throat. It was impossible. He was too strong. *There has to be a way...*

"Blaze... you don't want to do this..."

I could feel darkness creeping up on me, my consciousness slowly slipping through my fingers. But what really broke my heart were the dark blue flames burning in his eyes. Beneath the glassy façade of hypnosis, Blaze knew what he was doing to me—and he couldn't stop it.

It was up to me to put an end to it. Rewa's snickers reached my ears, as my eyes were beginning to roll back in my head. I found one last ounce of energy to look at her, and I realized that there was one way, one surefire way to stop Blaze, so I could get my lighters back from the ground where I'd dropped them when he'd first grabbed me.

My knee came up fast and rammed into his groin. His face contorted with pain, and he immediately let me go, falling to his knees. Both his hands covered the affected area. My legs were just as weak, and I nearly landed flat on my face, coughing and wheezing, my lungs readjusting to normal breathing.

"I am so sorry, Blaze," I whimpered, then looked around for my lighters, which were only a couple of feet away to my left. Blaze had rolled to his side in a fetal position.

I only had seconds before he'd recover and come at me again, Rewa's mind-bending still in full effect. With one last push, I managed to grab my lighters, then flipped them open as my gaze shifted to Rewa. That smug smile on her face vanished when she realized what was coming next.

"How's this for crispy?" I smirked, then shot out a flurry of fireballs at her and the other Lords.

She squealed, then dodged along with the others, my flames barely brushing them. I was too weak, still trying to come to my full senses. But Patrik reacted fast, just as Blaze was in the process of getting up. Patrick's fist nearly dislocated his jaw, but the impact was strong enough to knock him out.

He then helped me to my feet, firing blue flames at the Correction Officers coming at us.

"Make sure he stays down until we get out of here," he breathed, then went back to fighting more Maras.

I briefly shuddered, shaking my head in an attempt to regain my focus. The Lords were scrambling farther up the stairs, but none wanted to leave. They scowled at me and continued watching the fight. I wanted to go after them, but several Correction Officers reached me, and I had no choice but to focus on them.

Fortunately, not only was my inner fire itching to burn them all to a crisp, but the rest of my team was also kicking major ass. From the few glimpses I caught of Scarlett and Fiona, they were mowing Maras down like training dummies. I could hear bones breaking, yelps and screams of agonizing pain, and bodies hitting the ground, unable to withstand the strength and speed of the Novaks.

I slipped to the left, dodging the sword of a Correction Officer, and fashioned my own flaming blade, the incandescent concentration of pure fire that I'd recently learned to master. The Maras didn't want us dead, since they were after our souls —except Rewa, who had a bone to pick with me... I did hold hope that the other Lords would hold her back, though, since our souls were supposedly rare and "extra tasty". They were aiming to hurt us severely enough to allow our capture.

It gave me a slight advantage, as none of their hits were going for any of my vital organs. I, on the other hand, was going straight for the kill.

"Oh, no, you don't!" Avril's voice shot through.

I rammed my sword through a Mara, his flesh sizzling from the fire blade, his eyes popping out as he stared at me in disbelief. I kicked him back to retrieve my precious flaming weapon, then saw Avril and Heron joining the fight. They didn't stop to think. They simply reacted and started blocking hits, and chopping the limbs off any Maras who tried to get close to Blaze. Their orders were probably to snatch him while he was still unconscious.

"I'm not even going to ask what's going on here," Avril quipped, bringing her sword down on a Correction Officer. "But just so you know, the Maras are eating souls!"

Her opponent collapsed in a puddle of blood, and she didn't give him a chance to get back up. Her blade whistled through the air before it removed his head from the rest of his body.

"Yeah, we just figured it out ourselves," I shot back, dealing with my own side of hostiles.

Their numbers weren't shrinking fast enough, as more Correction Officers poured in from the upper levels, but we had enough anger pumping through our veins to take them all on, even without Blaze.

"So I take it we know who the bad guys are," Heron said sarcastically as he drove his sword through a Mara's neck, severing his spinal cord. Another came at him from behind, but Heron executed a swift and flawless hundred-and-eighty-degree turn with his blade perfectly angled to decapitate the Mara.

"And here I thought you were the slow one in the bunch," Avril snorted as they moved back to back, Correction Officers gathering around them like hungry vultures.

I almost smiled, but my new opponents were determined to keep me busy. I brought my flaming sword up, allowing it to cast its warm light on my face, before using it to bring death to the creatures that had so horribly betrayed us.

We had to get out of here, of course, but we also needed to leave them with enough casualties to keep them busy for the next couple of days, until we got a chance to regroup and once again come up with a new plan.

# 34

## FIONA

### (DAUGHTER OF BENEDICT & YELENA)

I had a bone to pick with Vincent. All these Correction Officers felt like annoying obstacles, since all I wanted to do was to look that bastard in the eyes and rip the heart right out of his chest. However, I wasn't getting much luck with getting closer to him. He and the Lords had weaseled farther away from the fight, taking refuge on the stairs, as they continued to watch the show.

Two Maras swung their swords at me. I shuffled back a couple of feet, then offered a vicious counterattack, slashing from a multitude of angles in a flurry of hits that eventually knocked one sword out of a Correction Officer's hand, briefly leaving me with just one armed opponent. I shoved my sword through his throat, then sliced outward, listening to the brief crackle of vertebrae separating.

He fell backward, and I quickly shifted my focus to the other Mara, who was halfway through getting his blade off the ground. Unfortunately for him, his position was perfect for a good old-fashioned decapitation. His head rolled, blood spreading at my feet, and I finally had a small window of opportunity to get to Vincent.

I dashed forward, prompting the Lords to jump back, but Vincent wasn't fast enough. With no intention of handling him right here, so close to Emilian and the others, where they could easily overpower me, I grabbed Vincent by the throat and swiftly pulled him back into the crowd of Correction Officers fighting the rest of my team.

He only managed to open his mouth as he brought his hands out to hit me. I punched him hard, crushing his left cheekbone. He grunted from the pain, but I wasn't done yet. He was stunned enough to get at least a dozen more punches right in the face—and I obliged. My knuckles were hurting, his sharp bones and even his teeth grazing them whenever I made contact.

But it didn't matter. This felt good...

"You made me think you were a good Mara," I growled, punching him again. "You passed yourself off as a decent creature. You lying piece of filth."

"Fiona, stop..." he managed, though he was close to losing consciousness. My strength was no match for his Mara nature, his abilities useless as long as my punches made his face tender, jostling his brain inside the skull.

"You thought you could get away with it. You still think you're going to get away with it, but rest assured, Vincent, that sooner or later you will leave this world a complete and utter failure," I hissed, ramming my fist into his stomach, just for the sake of diversity.

Blood gushed from his nose and mouth, red bruises blossoming on his rapidly swelling face. A scream broke my focus, and I looked up, my blood curdling as I watched Emilian mind-bending Imen into joining the fight.

"Ah, crap!" I groaned, then quickly shouted at Patrik: "Watch out, they're bringing Imen in! We'll have to be careful not to kill them."

"Then knock them unconscious we will!" Patrik shot back, before he set a Mara on blue fire.

I pulled my sword out—I'd put it away so I could handle Vincent hands-on—and brought the blade up to his throat. He whimpered, barely standing, wobbling and pleading for his life.

"Please, Fiona, please, don't do this... This isn't you!" he cried out.

"Well, it turns out this wasn't *you,* either!" I shot back.

I decided he wasn't worth keeping alive, so I pushed the sword a little deeper into his throat, drawing a droplet of blood. I was ready to end this. He caught me by surprise when he managed to pull a knife from the inside of his coat and stabbed me with it. He got my side, and the sharp pain quickly spread, white hot, through my torso.

"Aargh," I grunted, then cursed under my breath, my sword arm weakened in the process. It was enough for Vincent to slither out of my hold, sneering as he flipped the blade in his hand and prepared to strike again.

He charged at me, but he got himself violently halted by an invisible mass. The air rippled in front of me as Vincent landed on his side, smashing his head against the stairs. It wasn't enough to kill him, but it would keep him in bed for a long time. His blood glazed the stone steps as Rewa pulled him up to relative safety.

I understood then that the Lords didn't usually engage in combat. My first thought was that they weren't exactly trained into it. After all, they were, technically speaking, aristocrats, and they had plenty of Correction Officers and Imen to do their bidding for them.

My wound throbbed, and I held my side, staring at the air ripples in front of me, until I caught a glimpse of two red eyes. I froze, anticipating a blow powerful enough to knock me out cold. My hand gripped the sword, and I swung it out fast. The daemon blocked my hit, and sparks flew from where the blade had most likely hit a metal cuff.

"I just saved your life, and this is how you repay me?" Zane's voice knocked the air out of my lungs. Recovering, I breathed a sigh of relief.

"What in the world are you doing here?" I murmured.

Correction Officers came at us, but they were instantly screwed. Zane flashed between them, his claws or his blades cutting them open, before he literally ripped their heads off and tossed them aside like rotten watermelons.

He then got back to me, and I felt his hand touching my hip as he looked at my wound. With trembling fingers, I retrieved some of the healing herbs from one of my belt pockets, and quickly chewed on them.

"I'll be okay," I said, my mouth full.

"I have no doubt, now that *I'm* here," he replied, and I sensed the amusement in his voice.

"Seriously, though, what are you doing here? Also, you never told me you were a prince!" I shot back.

"Not sure you've noticed, but now is not the time for chitchat," he retorted. Zane was right, as much as I hated to admit it. My people were still outnumbered, despite their stellar ability to fight back. Blaze was still unconscious on the ground. And we *really* needed to get out of here.

"Why, thank you, Captain Redundant," I murmured.

"We can talk about my royal provenance later, beautiful," he replied, too softly for my comfort. "You need to get out, now. Take your team down the main road. Once you reach the plains, make a sharp turn left, right after the sign warning about the gorges. There's a small tunnel hidden beneath patches of purple flowers. There are Imen from the western plains there, waiting for you. They'll get you out of here and back with your friends."

"Whoa, how did that happen? Since when are you friends with the western plains Imen?"

"I really don't have time to explain this. Just do as I said," he scoffed, then took on another round of Correction Officers.

"Just don't hurt the Imen!" I shouted after him. "Their minds are bent; they don't know what they're doing!"

A Mara fell flat on the ground, his head separated from his body. Blood spurted out of his neck and spilled onto the cobblestone. Zane groaned, making sure that I heard his frustration, as he tackled another Mara while voicing his discontent toward my request.

"I swear, Fiona, you've already softened me up too much!"

I felt a smile tugging the corner of my mouth, but I brushed it aside and focused on getting my team out of here. I scanned the savage crowd, and caught a glimpse of Scarlett, Patrik, and the others.

But Zane wasn't the last surprise that our—hopefully—last night in Azure Heights offered. Sneaking up on a Correction Officer who was just about to pounce on Avril, Arrah swiftly grabbed his hair and pulled his head back, before cutting it off with a long, broad blade.

My heart skipped a beat, as I was genuinely happy and relieved to see the young Iman girl alive and well. And kicking her fair share of Mara ass.

"Arrah!" I called out, and she looked up at me, giving me a brief nod and a smile.

"Get your people out of here!" she replied. "Go to the western plains. I will see you later, I promise!"

I didn't get a chance to get closer to her. She got busy

fighting the Maras and knocking some of her own people out so they wouldn't get hurt, or worse, killed. Still, I was thrilled and suddenly energized to see that she had, in fact, kept her promise—though much later than I had hoped.

The truth was out now, but I was certain that she still had a lot to tell me.

I moved over to the edge of the terrace, getting ready to shout after Scarlett. She was fast enough to dart through the crowd and let the others know that it was time to retreat. I noticed another Correction Officer getting dangerously close to Blaze.

I dashed forward, using my full upper body to slam into the Mara and knock him down. Without giving him a chance to react, I took my sword out and ended him. A sharp clang caught my attention, somewhere to my right, as two blades clashed—one belonged to a Correction Officer, and one was wielded by Cadmus.

He briefly looked at me, frowning. "What are you waiting for? Get your dragon and get out of here!" he barked.

I didn't think twice about it. Equally thankful and surprised to see him fighting on our side, along with Arrah, I hoisted Blaze up and threw him over my shoulder. I stood, then whistled. Scarlett's head instantly turned, recognizing a sound we'd used since we were little girls to keep from losing each other in the redwood forests of The Shade.

"Get the others," I shouted. "We're busting out!"

She gave me a half-smile and a brief nod, then shot

through the crowd like the Bullet she was, and let Patrik, Caia, Avril, and Heron know that it was time to go. One by one, they killed off their opponents, then rushed after me before others could engage them further.

I ran the main road, while both Caia and Patrik shot a variety of fireballs at the Lords on the stairs above, to stop them from taking any action. Flames engulfed them, and they screamed and wailed. Several Correction Officers ran to their aid, knocking them down and patting the fires out.

We headed toward the lower level, light on our feet as the Maras still standing outside the infirmary came after us. Caia and Patrik continued to keep them at bay, one using her fire-power, while the other engaged in a series of Druid defense spells to help increase the distance between us and them.

"Where are we going?" Scarlett asked, as she ran by my side.

"There's a tunnel down there, with Imen from the western plains waiting to take us to Harper," I replied, holding an unconscious Blaze over my shoulders.

"Was there a daemon back there?" Avril huffed.

"Yup. That was Zane. Helping us. Still wrapping my head around that one, but he's the one who told me about the tunnel." I chuckled.

Despite everything that had just happened—all the fighting, the anger, and the betrayal—I couldn't help but breathe easier, now that we were getting as far away from Azure Heights as possible.

"And was that Cadmus lending us a hand?" Heron added.

"And Arrah." I nodded, my heart beating a little faster as the warning sign Zane had mentioned came into view, just fifty yards away. "Turns out we're not all helpless and without allies in this world, huh?"

"Yeah, you can definitely say that again!" Scarlett replied.

Somehow, I picked up speed, despite my heavy load. Just the thought of reaching the western plains and getting back to Harper and the others seemed to give me the extra boost I needed. We'd made it this far, and I sure as hell wasn't going to let those soul-eating bastards from either species beat us. My key takeaway from that whole ordeal was the confirmation that there was a swamp witch on Neraka.

Once we regrouped and put together a proper action plan, I knew exactly what our main objective was. It was as clear as my eagerness to ultimately crush Vincent's skull upon our next encounter.

*We find the swamp witch, and we put an end to this.*

## 35

---

# AVRIL

(DAUGHTER OF LUCAS & MARION)

I'd gone from horrified to surprisingly optimistic in less than an hour. After Heron and I had witnessed the Mara nurses feeding off the souls of Imen back in the infirmary, and after we'd killed the ones who'd thought they were strong enough to take us on, I had felt queasy.

But then, upon returning to the front of the building to find Correction Officers attacking our team, I had to shove all that aside and focus on getting ourselves out of there. I quickly made the link to what we'd seen in the infirmary, the rest of the puzzle pieces falling into place afterward.

I knew we'd have some time later in the night to fully process everything, so, in the meantime, I ran alongside Fiona and Scarlett, with Caia, Patrik, and Heron right behind us, and Blaze unconscious over Fiona's shoulder.

"We caught a Mara nurse feeding on an Iman's soul," I told Fiona as we reached the gorge warning sign and made a sharp turn to the left. I could hear the Maras shouting and rumbling down the main road, but Patrik and Caia had done a good job of keeping them away. Just as our feet sank into the tall grass at the base of the mountain, Patrik shot out a flurry of blue fires and white sparks, leaving our pursuers dazed and unable to see where we went. "Sorry we took a while to get back—we had to deal with her and her colleagues."

"That's cool, I figured you were caught up," Fiona breathed, leading us farther along the mountain base.

"I can't believe this is happening," I replied. "I mean, I do believe it, but still... wow. Just, wow!"

"What the hell were they thinking, though? Luring us here like that?" Caia muttered.

"I have no idea, but I think the western tribe will be able to tell us more," I said.

"Or Zane." Fiona narrowed her eyes as she looked ahead. "Lord Kifo clearly can't. You heard the Lords. The poor guy, it's why he's been trying to warn us since we first got here!"

Two dark figures emerged from a patch of purple flower bushes, their big, round eyes glimmering with what looked like relief, as they beamed their smiles at us. They were two young Imen boys, maybe sixteen years old, covered in brown leathers and dark green capes. The orange dots on their temples caught my eye.

"You made it!" one of them exclaimed.

"Yeah, sorry we're late. It got... busy up there," Fiona replied as we all came to a halt.

"I'm Alles, and this is Dion," the young Iman said. "Vesta and Miss Hellswan sent us. I take it you have a better idea of what's going on now?"

"Sort of, but I'm sure Vesta will fill in the blanks. In the meantime, we need to go. Now."

They both nodded and motioned for us to follow them. They disappeared beneath the flower bushes, and we went in after them. A tunnel opened before us, its walls covered in red clay. One by one, we snuck through, and the Imen boys led us down into a loop, then a straight line beneath the two-mile plain.

"Patrik, can you make sure they don't follow us through here?" I asked the Druid.

He gave me a brief nod when I glanced over my shoulder at him, then muttered a spell and reached his hands out, his fingers brushing against the walls on both sides. They left incandescent green traces, which quickly turned to massive cracks that collapsed the structure behind us with a deafening rumble.

We kept running, the Imen boys right in front of us.

"How do you two know Zane?" Fiona asked.

"Who?" Dion replied, his breath short.

"The daemon who sent us down here in the first place. How do you two know him?"

"We don't! Not personally, anyway," Dion explained. "We'd

just made it out of the tunnel and were on our way up, when he popped up out of nowhere and started questioning us, asking what we were doing there. Our first instinct was to run, but... let's just say he was faster."

"And convincing," Alles muttered. "We thought he was going to kill us, until we all heard the fighting upstairs. We'd never seen a prince of daemons up close before, you see. We certainly didn't expect him to tell us to wait by the tunnel. It was weird, neither Dion nor I could understand what was going on."

"Then he said that he'd send you all down here, for us to take you out of the city," Dion added. "He said he didn't care who we were or what we were doing there, anyway. He just wanted us to get you all to safety. So, you know, we watched him turn invisible before he went up to the infirmary. He's not the first daemon we've had help from, but he's definitely the first prince. The tides are changing..."

"That is just so sweet!" I chuckled, then grunted as Fiona nudged me with her elbow.

"We have two indigo horses with us," Dion then said. "Two of you can get on them, with us, and we'll lead the way through the Valley of Screams. The daemons are still recovering after what your friends did to them."

"We barely saw any of them out in the gorges earlier," Alles chuckled. "Whatever damage your friends caused, it'll take them some time to get over."

"Good, it means the gorges won't be much trouble tonight,"

Fiona muttered. "Caia and Blaze here will join you on the horses. The rest of us can keep up without a problem."

I could still hear the commotion behind us. The Maras had tracked us to the tunnel, but they were stuck on the other side.

"There are about eighty feet of dirt and rocks between us and them," Patrik said. "They've got their work cut out for them. We'll reach the ravine long before they can even get past the blockage."

I gave him a brief thumbs-up, then followed Fiona and the Imen boys as the tunnel began its smooth ascension toward the surface. We made it out into a narrow ravine, with maybe twenty feet of space between its tall limestone walls. Two indigo horses waited by a sharp rock poking out from the ground, and the Imen boys got on them. Caia climbed onto Dion's horse, while Fiona plopped Blaze behind Alles, using a rope to hold him in place, tied to the saddle.

"Just make sure you don't lose him along the way," Fiona muttered. "We can't do much without our dragon."

Alles's eyes grew wide with surprise, and he stared at Blaze. "This is the dragon?"

"Yeah, he's out of it for the time being," Fiona replied.

"Why? What happened to him?"

"He got all... murderous..." Caia sighed, her expression pained as she glanced at Blaze, whose large body was bent over the horse's hindquarters.

"The Maras mind-bent him," I clarified.

Alles and Dion nudged the horses with their heels, and the

creatures darted forward. We followed, keeping up as we moved through the zigzagging ravine, the first moon glowing overhead.

My heart was tight beneath my ribs, my stomach tiny and stressed, but my muscles worked just fine as I dashed through the gorge. I started going over all the events that had occurred since we'd first set foot on Neraka, and the little inconsistencies I'd noticed before started to find their places in the much clearer picture of Azure Heights I now had.

This was a nasty place, inhabited by horrible creatures who had not only failed to better their ways, but had in fact gone from bad to worse. Like a plague, they'd decimated the native population of Imen, feeding off their blood and their souls.

I knew our only hope of defeating both the Maras and the daemons rested in our ability to find the swamp witch. As Fiona and I briefly glanced at each other, I knew we were on the same page. One way or another, we were going to be the end of the Exiled Maras.

Looking at it from an objective, exploratory perspective, the daemons were natives. We had no right to wipe them off the face of Neraka altogether, but we could force them into submission so they'd back off the Imen. But the Maras were foreign agents, already an anomaly in the Nerakian environment.

The damage they were doing was almost irreversible. They

didn't deserve a second chance. *They've already wasted their second chance...*

# 36

# HARPER

## (DAUGHTER OF HAZEL & TEJUS)

Jax and Hansa were talking to Vesta on the other side of the campfire, while Amund, Eristhena, and Ledda retreated to the main tent to further discuss the recent developments, along with my request to release Caspian.

I stayed by his cage, both of us sitting back to back, leaning against the iron bars. The Imen guards kept a distance of ten feet on each side, somewhat comfortable that I was there to keep an eye on him. Their fear of him at this point felt unjustified, but I hadn't spent the last few thousands of years fighting against his species. I did understand their wariness. It ran deep and across multiple generations.

"I am sorry, Miss Hellswan," Caspian murmured after a long silence. "I can't say it enough."

"Had you not been under the blood oath, would you have

told us?" I asked, my gaze wandering across the camp. Females herded their children to a large dinner table, while the males added more wood to the fire and helped serve the food. They seemed to have a good balance as a tribe, their bonds tight and powerful—I could tell from the looks they gave each other, flickers of unconditional love and affection lighting their faces up.

"From the moment you'd set foot on Neraka," Caspian replied. The rawness in his husky voice made my skin tingle. I knew he meant it.

"Then there's nothing to apologize for." I sighed. "It's not your fault. You were born in a society of degenerates, and you tried your best to make things right."

"The Kifo line has always been... complicated," he said. "Those who wanted to do good... they paid the price."

I heard him groan, then quickly turned around to see smoke rising from his face. He was trying to tell me part of the truth, doing his best to find some kind of loophole in the blood oath. "Lord Kifo, please," I breathed. "You'll hurt yourself. Stop it."

"I just want to tell you the truth," he murmured, turning so he could face me. The red blotches on his cheeks were already healing, and the earlier burns were long gone. Had he not stopped when he did, he would've turned to ashes. The pain in his jade eyes clawed at my heart, but there wasn't much I could do for him at this point.

"You will, someday." I gave him a soft smile. "Once we get

the swamp witch back, she'll be able to break the oath. I hope. I don't know... This is dark stuff they've put on you. The books we have from the swamp witches have yet to be fully translated. Maybe in a couple of months, but we don't have that kind of time. And it's absolutely futile if we're stuck here, with no access to Calliope, which is where we keep the books, in the first place."

"I trust you'll succeed." He nodded. "I've never met anyone as determined as yourself, Miss Hellswan."

He warmed me up on the inside with just a handful of words. How could I deny what I was feeling for him, when his effect on me was so obvious? I'd stopped trying to fool myself, anyway. From the moment I'd learned about his full knowledge of the Maras' plans, I'd experienced the pain of heartbreak, subsequently followed by the relief at learning about his blood oath—it didn't make things easier for our mission, but at least it cleared him of any wrongdoing.

Whatever he had or hadn't done, it was all because of the oath, and his desire to survive. There had to be a way out for him, somehow. He'd already betrayed his people for me, for us, and, most importantly, for freedom and peace. My heart grew a couple of sizes whenever I looked at him.

An idea crossed through my head as we gazed at each other, the cold iron bars between us.

"What if... What if I ask you questions, and you blink. Once for yes, twice for no. Want to try it?" I asked.

He gave me a weak smile, then exhaled sharply and moved

closer, so only a few inches were left between us. My pulse went on its usual rampage caused by the close proximity, but I held on for dear life, trying to keep my cool in front of him.

"Worth a shot, I think," he replied softly.

"Okay, here goes... Let's start with a simple question. Was your ancestor, Teller Kifo, a part of the effort to enslave the Imen and drink their blood?"

He blinked twice. A couple of seconds went by as we waited for his skin to sizzle, but nothing happened. Suddenly, hope started blossoming in my chest. I took a deep breath and smiled.

"No. Okay. I'll go ahead and guess that Teller Kifo was one of the Exiled Maras who truly repented and wanted his people to start a new, better life on Neraka," I replied. "Your parents, were they on board with what the Lords were doing? The soul-eating? The exsanguination?"

He blinked twice again, his gaze dropping to the ground as an aura of dark, deep red enveloped him. I had a feeling I'd finally identified some of his emotions. What I was seeing in this moment had to be grief... longing for his mother and father.

"And your adoptive father, Dillon? Was he a soul-eater?"

Caspian blinked twice once more, prompting me to nod slowly.

"Did the Lords kill your parents and Dillon, then? Because they didn't want to comply, maybe?"

One blink, and my heart felt like an open wound. *Oh, the poor thing...*

"You mean to tell me that they killed your parents, then your adoptive father, but they've not scared you into willfully joining their agenda?"

He blinked once.

"They don't deserve you," I replied. "Caspian, I understand why you did what you did. Taking a blood oath and keeping quiet was better than losing your life over their greed and hubris."

"Thank you," he murmured, his eyes drilling into me, a vague smile stretching his lips.

"As inconvenient as it may be, I'm glad you took the blood oath," I said, not sure whether I had the courage to finish that statement. After everything we'd been through, it would've been a shame not to be honest about what I was feeling. "Otherwise we never would've met."

"When you put it like that, I can't help but agree, Miss Hellswan." His gaze softened.

I watched as little tendrils of gold emerged from him. They spread around in a diffused shimmer, covering the grief he'd exhibited until now. I couldn't help but wonder what that feeling was—it only appeared when he looked at me.

Caspian couldn't tell me the truth about his people because of a blood oath. The least I could do was tell him *my* truth, because I could. It took me another minute to summon the courage to speak up, but when I did, it was impossible to stop myself.

"Caspian, I need to tell you something."

"I'm listening," he replied, his voice low. He refused to take his eyes off me.

"Remember when you gave me your blood to heal my wounds, back in the gorges?"

"How could I possibly forget?"

"Oh, right, the accidental Pyrope," I murmured. "Right. Well, it did something to me. You know that, as a sentry, I am able to read emotions, among other things. I never could do that with a Mara, though. However, after I drank your blood... well, I started seeing colors emanating from your body. I can literally see your emotions. I don't know what they all mean yet. My parents tell me everyone experiences things differently, especially across species. So I don't yet know how to identify what you feel in various moments, but I think I'm starting to get the hang of it."

He stilled, his expression unchanged. He listened quietly as I went on, slowly cocking his head to the side, and I felt my blood simmer under his gaze. This intensity between us was bound to eventually burn me alive, figuratively speaking. My only hope was that I wouldn't end up with a tattered heart. I'd gotten a taste earlier with all the revelations, and it had hurt like hell. I was in no way ready for more of *that*.

"What have you gotten the hang of, exactly?" he asked.

"The dark red you had earlier, for example, when I

mentioned your parents and Dillon. I think it's grief. Longing, maybe," I muttered, my attention faltering, as the gold around him seemed brighter than before. The more I looked at it, the more intense it became, to the point where I shifted my focus back to his hypnotizing jade eyes just so I wouldn't have to narrow mine.

"I think you got that right," he replied, inching closer. My lungs faltered, and I held my breath.

"And now there's a golden aura of sorts," I continued, my voice barely audible. "You only have that when you look at me, though. I don't know what it is... or why. Just thought you should know."

He blinked slowly, while I bit my lower lip, afraid to say anything else. He'd yet to tell me how he felt about my ability to read him. My biggest fear was that he'd consider it a gross invasion of his privacy, and that would be a massive bummer, since I had no way of turning this off.

"I think I know what it is," he whispered.

"I... I mean, I don't want you to think I'm going to use this knowledge against you," I stuttered, unable to recognize myself for a split second. "I can't turn it off. And I'm... I'm still learning to interpret the colors. I really don't know what the gold stands for."

"I'll show you," he breathed. His gaze darkened and burned green at the same time. My body bucked as he reached out—his hand gripping the back of my neck—pulled me close, and kissed me.

The iron bars were far enough apart for our heads to fit, but I lost all sense of anything material as his mouth covered mine. My lips parted in response, and I welcomed him with a soft moan as he deepened the kiss and my mind scattered across the universe.

Heat expanded through me, as if I were a newborn star. The golden shimmer I'd seen around me covered my field of vision as I closed my eyes and surrendered to Caspian. His tongue slipped through, touching mine as our lips fused.

The world around us disappeared, and I understood what he'd meant. That gold—it was the same that Serena had described surrounding Draven. Their closeness, the affection, the attraction, the unstoppable magnetism... It was all there, but between Caspian and me. I wasn't the only one falling. He was experiencing the same internal storms—I could almost feel them, echoing beneath my ribcage.

I couldn't get enough of him, and it seemed he felt the same, as he intensified our kiss. My arms slipped into the cage, snaking around his neck, and I pulled myself closer to him.

It was slightly uncomfortable, but neither of us seemed to mind. We abandoned everything and held each other against the iron bars. We kissed as if the world were about to end and start anew at the same time.

I understood then how badly I'd wanted this to happen.

# 37

## HARPER

### (DAUGHTER OF HAZEL & TEJUS)

I rested my head against his as we held each other close— or, at least, as close as we could, given the iron cage between us. Caspian's eyes were filled with the same kind of warmth that seemed to emanate from within me.

My breath was ragged, and my heart was still in the middle of extraordinarily agile somersaults. His gaze found my lips again, and clouds gathered beneath his long black eyelashes.

"Miss Hellswan, I'm afraid I'm in very deep trouble," he murmured, then ran his fingers through my hair, before returning to trace the contours of my face. His touch alone had the power to dismantle me completely, breaking me down to a subatomic level.

"Harper, please," I whispered. "I think we're past the stage of addressing each other by our last names."

"Harper." He smiled gently, turning me into a melting blob of wax.

I brought my hand up, my index and middle finger brushing against his chin, as I relished the feel of him somewhere deep in my bones. "Caspian," I breathed. "What are we going to do with... with this?"

He let out a long, tortured sigh, his thumb passing over my lower lip.

"I don't know," he said. "But I've been finding myself inexplicably drawn to you, Harper, and I wouldn't want it any other way."

"We'll get through this," I replied, my resolve bubbling back to the surface. "I'll find the swamp witch and set you free. We'll reach out to my people, and..."

My voice trailed off as I realized what I was about to say. Caspian gave me a weak, sad smile as he finished my sentence. "And you'll obliterate the Exiled Maras. Perfectly understandable."

"They're your people. I'm sorry. But it has to be done."

"I completely agree. I just want you to know that they're not all like that. There are some, still in Azure Heights, who've been forced under a blood oath," he replied, grimacing from the pain as red burns emerged on his forehead.

I cupped his face with my hands, pressing my lips tight together. "Stop it, Caspian. I can't bear to see you in pain. Just don't."

"Look at you, so soft and... sweet." He smirked, then kissed the tip of my nose, his hot breath tickling my face. "I never could've guessed, with all your layers of badassery."

I chuckled lightly, noticing the shift between us. The tension between us was still very much there, just as intense, if not more so. But we had a name for it. We knew what we were dealing with. With one kiss, we'd managed to identify the invisible strings connecting our very souls. We'd yet to say the name out loud, but I knew we would, soon enough.

"Harper!"

Avril's voice startled me. I instantly shot to my feet, my heart drumming as I saw Avril and the rest of my team, back in one piece. Blaze was barely standing, leaning against Caia with one arm around her shoulder. He seemed quite out of it, but alive.

I dashed over to them, just as Jax and Hansa joined in. We hugged one another for what seemed like an eternity, a wave of relief washing over me as I held them, alive and well, in my arms.

"Thank the Daughters!" Hansa exclaimed as she took Fiona in her arms.

"It's so good to see you all," I croaked, tears coming up to my eyes. After everything we'd been through, it was truly blissful to see us all back together. Avril hugged me again, kissing my forehead like the sweet, older sort-of-sister that she was.

"What happened to him?" Jax nodded at Blaze, who was

looking around, visibly dazed and confused, as if waking up from a dream.

"Rewa mind-bent him," Caia explained briefly. "He started choking me, so..."

"We had to neutralize him, so to speak." Patrik shrugged, then patted the dragon on the shoulder. "He'll be okay, though. Some food and some sleep, and he'll be good as new in the morning."

"What happened?" I asked, as Vesta motioned for her two Imen boys to fetch some water and blood. Hansa and Jax had taken care of dinner for us vampires, after the Imen had been kind enough to give us two large animals. Hansa had filled a couple of jugs, enough to go around.

"We told the Lords about Darius and the king, but we never mentioned Shaytan by his name," Caia said.

"Until Emilian did." Patrik smirked. "It all unraveled then. Avril and Heron caught Mara nurses feeding on Imen. We were surrounded by Correction Officers. We had to get out, of course."

"Zane helped us," Fiona added. "And Arrah, too. I think we'll see her on this side of the gorges soon enough."

"And Cadmus," Avril said. "That was unexpected, but more than welcome. It took us a while to get out of there with Blaze out cold, but we did it. We found Dion and Alles at the tunnel entrance, and, well, here we are."

"Together again." I grinned, then briefly glanced over my shoulder at Caspian. He stood quietly in his cage, smiling at me. He seemed just as relieved as I was, and for good reason, too. Our team was whole again.

We sat closer to the campfire as Dion and Alles brought over pitchers of water and blood. Vesta took a seat next to Hansa, and we brought Avril and the others up to speed on everything we'd discovered, without skimping on the details.

They completed our accounts with what they'd seen and heard in Azure City, and we all came to the same conclusion. The decision was unanimous.

"We need to find the swamp witch." Patrik nodded slowly, his knee gently brushing against Scarlett, whose cheeks had blossomed in an adorable shade of pink. I looked around and realized that a lot had changed between the members of our team, during the time I'd been away and stuck in the daemon city.

The dynamic was shifting, not just between Caspian and me or Hansa and Jax. Patrik and Scarlett seemed different, and even Blaze and Caia exchanged some peculiar glances. It kind of made sense—not just because of the natural chemistry, but because of all our trials and tribulations. The mess we'd found ourselves thrown into had inadvertently brought us closer together.

And I was counting on this internal change for what lay ahead.

"Caia, I'm so sorry," Blaze finally spoke, his gaze a bit more focused.

"There he is! Welcome back!" Heron grinned.

"I'm... I'm so sorry. I don't know how... I couldn't stop myself," Blaze murmured, and Caia took his hands in hers, giving him a warm, broad smile.

"Listen, it's okay," she said softly. "It wasn't your fault. We all know it. *I* know it. Mind-bending is a powerful thing."

"I could've killed you."

"You didn't!" Caia insisted, cupping his face in an attempt to make him feel better.

"Besides, she kicked you in the nuts, man. Consider the price paid for that," Heron quipped, and we all laughed lightly.

"It's okay," Caia reassured Blaze, and he nodded slowly, looking at us.

"What do we do now?" he asked.

A couple of seconds went by before Jax cleared his throat and straightened his back to get our full attention.

"Well, our first objective, at this point, is to get into the daemon city up north and find out where they're keeping what's left of the Druid delegation. Especially the swamp witch," he said.

"I will take you there," Vesta said. "I know two daemons there, pacifists, who can help us. One can help us get in. I've already sent word to him to let him know we're coming. He knows the city inside and out, and can help us move around undetected. The second is the one with the answers you seek regarding the Exiled Maras and the daemons' plans to bring more of your kind here."

"Oh, you mean replenish their food source," Fiona muttered, gritting her teeth. Her anger was mirrored in all of us. I felt it twisting my stomach in painful knots, and, just like Fiona, I looked forward to snapping some Exiled Mara necks. In fact, we all did.

"We'll leave at dawn," Jax continued. "Eat, drink, and rest, in the meantime. As soon as the sun is up, we're out of here. It's imperative that we find the swamp witch. She can help us break every single disruption spell that these bastards have set up. Once we reach out and alert Calliope, it'll be the end of the Exiled Maras."

"The daemons are temporarily weakened after what we did to them," Hansa added. "However, that is just one city. They will get reinforcements. And when they do, they'll be coming for us. I think the Maras will do the same. I'm worried they might be able to follow our tracks here."

"They won't, Hansa," Vesta assured her. "My people will move farther to the west as soon as we leave. I've already confirmed this with Amund. Besides, I told you, we have a few good tricks up our sleeves when it comes to eluding those creeps—it's how we've managed to survive until now."

"We need allies, in the meantime," I said. "We're on our own, and, dragon or not, we have to get some strength in numbers. Enough to hold out until we find the swamp witch and contact Draven and GASP."

"There are some creatures still living in this world," Vesta murmured. "They're almost extinct, though. We haven't seen most of them in years. But there are rumors, whispers flying across the western meadows. We can try and reach out to them. I can send a couple of scouts, if you'd like. If they see people rising against the daemons, and if they see you, they might be interested in joining the fight. This is our world, too."

"Thank you, Vesta, that would be a great idea." Jax nodded his approval. "Hopefully, they'll let Lord Kifo out by morning, as well. We need him."

"I believe they will," the water fae replied.

They had to. I wasn't going to leave him behind. I looked over my shoulder again. Caspian was sitting by the iron bars of his cage, his gaze fixed on me as he listened intently. He gave me a nod and a discreet smile, his jade eyes flickering with newfound resolve. I mirrored that perfectly.

Come morning, we were going to dig deeper into the world of daemons, then reclaim the freedom of the Imen and stop this soul-eating madness, once and for all. We'd been deceived and betrayed by the Exiled Maras—and their punishment was going to be swift, unforgiving, and, this time, final.

They'd been spared once. We had no intention of making that mistake again.

Not when the lives of so many innocent people were at stake, along with our own. No way in hell would I let them lure more GASP agents to Neraka, just so they could fulfill their insane fantasy of replenishing their soul food supply.

The soul was never meant to be treated like this. Life deserved more respect than what the daemons and Exiled

Maras were showing. And I was going to make sure they learned this lesson the hard way.

# 38

## DEREK

We'd been planning an expansion for The Shade since the Daughters of Eritopia had established a permanent portal between our worlds. With the influx of Eritopians visiting our beautiful island, we'd finally reached the point where we simply needed more space. We'd built as many cabins and treehouses and townhouses as we could on the mainland—if we permitted more construction, things would start to feel cluttered, and I was not going to let that happen. With so many supernaturals inhabiting our land, it was vital we all have ample open space to stretch our legs... or wings, as the case may be.

"Honestly, I expected this day to come a lot sooner," Eli remarked, standing to my right at the end of the Port's jetty. He was holding a large scroll of paper which contained the proposed layout of the artificial extension we were planning to build out over the ocean, side by side with the Port. His wife Shayla, Ibrahim, Corrine, Kiev, and Mona were also with us, examining the ocean that stretched out within The Shade's protective barrier. Eli and the witches made up the core of our expansion team—Eli being lead architect—while Kiev, having some downtime, had tagged along with his wife.

"Me too," Ibrahim said. "Ever since GASP replaced the IBSI."

I nodded. That had been a significant milestone in The Shade's growth, to say the least. Before defeating Atticus Conway and becoming the official protective agency for Earth, we had made official alliances with the dragons, white witches, and jinn—which increased our population, as a significant number of them came to live with us—but in taking the IBSI down, we had formed further alliances with the werewolves, Hawks, and ogres, which just added to our "zoo", as Corrine fondly referred to it.

Then came our Nevertide excursion, which had brought in an influx of sentries, and most recently Eritopia, which had opened up a whole other Pandora's box of diverse creatures, many of which I hadn't even known existed: Maras, Druids, incubi, succubi... Yes. It was time.

I couldn't deny, though, that I felt a stab of melancholy at the prospect. No, building an extension over the ocean would not really alter the main island, but still, it was a sign of change. And with change came the bitter-sweetness of nostalgia, of times lost and gone, never to be returned to.

I couldn't help but think back to how The Shade was... before it was even The Shade. Centuries ago, when I'd first discovered it, that fateful day my ship had washed ashore. It was just a wild island back then, inhabited only by the local animals. And we were just a handful of vampires. Me, my sister, brother, father, Xavier, Cameron, Liana, Eli, Claudia, Kyle, Sam, and some others, many of whom we'd lost along the way. Then there was Cora, followed by her successor Corrine, and the humans we began kidnapping.

As much as those times had been filled with struggle and heartache, I wouldn't have traded them for the world. Not just because the circumstances had brought Sofia to me, but because they'd shaped me into the person I was today. A man I could comfortably look at in the mirror—which was a lot more than I could say for myself before.

As I looked at the plans Eli was holding, I realized that watching The Shade grow was like watching a child grow. I guessed, because it was my child, in a way. I'd founded it, then fought to protect and preserve it for the past... almost six hundred years now.

"God, I feel old," I muttered, breaking the quiet that had descended on us. The feeling was not exactly helped by the fact that I sensed one day very soon I was going to become a great-great-grandfather...

Corrine smiled wryly. "Ah, Derek." She reached out and patted me on the shoulder. "I know. This *is* a nostalgic time, isn't it? Just take comfort in the fact that Kiev is way older."

The green-eyed vampire threw Corrine a scowl. "You're not exactly a spring chick, witch."

Mona prodded him. "I thought we talked about you calling your son's mother-in-law that."

"What? Chick or witch?"

Corrine snorted, while Mona and Ibrahim rolled their eyes.

I chuckled. Even after decades of being co-in-laws, Corrine still hadn't gotten tired of taking pokes at Kiev.

Eli cleared his throat, straightening the plan he was holding. "So... this is our first solid draft. For now, what I really want is comments on the size of the platform. Do we start smaller and see how we do? Or larger than we think we might need? I mean, The Shade's population is only going to continue to grow, so it's probably almost impossible to build something too large. We want to accommodate at least a hundred houses at first, and since this area will be mostly inhabited by Eritopians, I'm thinking—"

"Derek!" I heard Sofia calling my name from behind us.

I turned and saw her approaching with Draven. I'd left her in the Great Dome with Rose and River, where they'd been talking about extensions for The Shade's school, so I was surprised to see her approaching now—especially with Draven. Even from this distance, I could see that her face was concerned, which unnerved me.

"Draven?" Eli narrowed his eyes, spotting the Master Druid of Calliope, too.

We left the jetty and walked toward them.

"Sorry to come all the way here and disturb you," Draven said as he reached us, bowing curtly. His manners always surprised me—Serena had married an absolute gentleman. *Thank the stars.*

"Is something wrong?" I asked.

"Not exactly." Draven shook his head. "The team on Neraka is okay. I just spoke to them. Not even worried about Tenebris anymore; the boys there are doing an excellent job of dismantling the rebel groups. But Serena and I have been digging through the Druid Archives, and... well, we've found an inconsistency."

"What kind of inconsistency?" I asked.

"The Druid delegation that was traveling in the area close to Neraka, the one we assumed had crash-landed there... they never came back," Draven explained. "I checked the coordinates over and over, and the records, too. It's the only delegation that vanished."

"But Rewa said they bid them farewell and watched them fly off in their light orb," Sofia murmured, looking at me, the wariness in her eyes evident.

"Do you think the Exiled Maras lied?" Corrine asked, frowning.

"I'm not sure, but yes, I am considering that possibility," he replied.

"To what end, though? I'm not sure I get it," Kiev muttered, scratching his stubbled chin as he pursed his lips.

"Again, I do not know at this point." Draven shrugged. "But, like I said, the team was okay. I checked in via Telluris, and they were still in the gorges, investigating. They've yet to uncover the mystery behind all those disappearances."

"I doubt they'll find out that quickly. It's only, what... day three?" Ibrahim raised an eyebrow, and Draven responded with a brief nod before shifting his focus back to me.

I wasn't really sure what to make of this. If the Exiled Maras had lied about the Druid delegation, it didn't look good for them. Most importantly, it put the GASP team we'd sent over at risk. But the delegation could also have disappeared after they'd left Neraka. Without more information, it was difficult to draw any final conclusions. I couldn't even consider any kind of action in response to either possibility, because it was simply too soon.

"I think we should give the exploratory team a couple more days to do some more digging into the disappearances," I concluded after a long moment. "Let's see what findings they come up with. The Maras might not even know that the Druid delegation never returned to Calliope. It would cause a diplomatic mess if we started suspecting the victims of proven crimes of wrongdoings of their own, at least at this point in time."

"I must say, I agree," Eli added. "We could reconvene in a couple of days, while you keep in touch with the Neraka team. We can decide on a course of action then, once we learn more about what's going on there with all the disappearances."

"I understand." Draven nodded. "I was also thinking I could tell Jax to ask the Five Lords to give him an account of what they saw when they bid the Druid delegation farewell. You know, just to fish for details. They might hold important clues and not even know it, if we go on the presumption of innocence."

"That makes sense," I replied. "Just make sure he's... gentle about it. I think the team's findings regarding the abductions are essential right now. The sooner they discover the culprits, the sooner they'll come back to us. Frankly, I'm not at all comfortable with them so far away, with just Telluris as a means of communication and just a swamp witch spell for interstellar travel."

Sofia wrapped her arms around my waist and pulled herself closer to my side. I knew she felt the same way. As proud as we were of our younglings, and regardless of the immovable faith we had in their abilities, neither of us was truly comfortable with the risks they were exposing themselves to in a completely foreign world.

I wanted to see them all back, sooner rather than later.

"Draven," I added, "can you do me a favor?"

He raised his eyebrows. "Yes?"

"Do you have any way of looking into that galaxy as a whole?" I asked. "One of our witches will help you, if needed. I want you to analyze it. I know we can't see Neraka because of whatever weird effect that asteroid belt has on the planet's visibility in space, but you should still be able to see the rest of that solar system."

"I see where you're going with this," Draven replied with a nod and a confident half-smile. "We can study the galaxy and get a better idea of what that part of the In-Between is like, even from afar. Whatever dwells on Neraka could also be found on neighboring planets."

"Exactly. Consider it research," I said.

"Leave it to me." He bowed again, then turned around and walked back to the Dome, while Sofia remained with me.

We watched him as he gradually became a small dot at the end of the sandy beach, and a sliver of unease crept up to my throat, clutching tightly as I swallowed. It was too soon to draw any conclusions regarding Neraka, I reminded myself. But, still, as a great-grandfather and, most importantly, as the leader of GASP, I worried about my people.

The possibility of Exiled Maras lying about the Druid delegation didn't sit well with me. However, we didn't know for certain that they'd deceived us. I disliked this kind of decision limbo, but right now, I didn't have much choice.

A couple more days, and we'd take another look at what was going on there, and Draven would keep in close contact with them via Telluris.

In the meantime, I could focus on this development project... while secretly pondering worst-case scenarios regarding Neraka.

# READY FOR THE NEXT PART OF THE SHADIANS' STORY?

Dear Shaddict,

Thank you for reading A City of Lies!

The next book in the series, **ASOV 56: A League of Exiles**, releases **February 19th, 2018**!

Visit www.bellaforrest.net for details on ordering your copy.

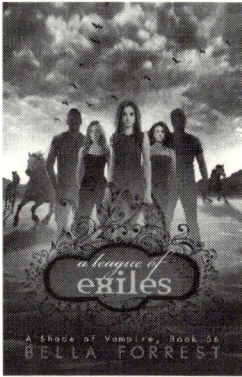

I'll see you there!

Love,

Bella x

P.S. Join my VIP email list and I'll send you a personal reminder as soon as I have a new book out. Visit here to sign up: **www.forrestbooks.com**

(Your email will be kept 100% private and you can unsubscribe at any time.)

P.P.S. Follow The Shade on Instagram and check out some of the beautiful graphics: @ashadeofvampire

You can also come say hi on Facebook: www.facebook.com/AShadeOfVampire

And Twitter: @ashadeofvampire